The Berlin assignment given to Sterling, an aircraft engineer, seemed simple enough. His mission—to interrogate a captive scientist brought from East Germany by Intelligence agents and return home. But he finds himself in the midst of a shadow war of espionage, involved in a brutal political murder and, because of his love for his beautiful German "house-keeper", dragged further into the web of danger and intrigue. This fast-moving, suspenseful novel is all the more startling because it is based on fact. It's events parallel to-day's newspaper headlines.

To Winnie,
with love

A Consul Book

The Berlin Couriers

JAMES McGOVERN

Published by

WORLD DISTRIBUTORS (MANCHESTER) LTD.

LONDON—MANCHESTER

ENGLAND

This *CONSUL* edition, complete and unabridged,
published in England, 1961, by

WORLD DISTRIBUTORS (MANCHESTER) Ltd., 36 GREAT RUSSELL STREET, LONDON, W.C.1.

Copyright © 1960 James McGovern

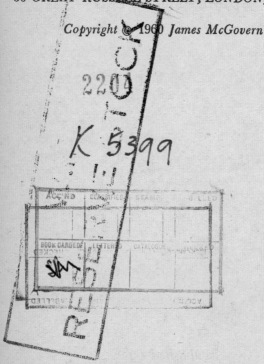
PRINTED IN GREAT BRITAIN
BY CHARLES BIRCHALL & SONS, LTD.,
LIVERPOOL AND LONDON

PART ONE

The Apprentice Agent

1

IT WAS dusk of a lovely June afternoon in 1953. The stewardess shook his shoulder—they were approaching Tempelhof Airport. Peter Sterling roused himself from a bad dream to glance down at silver lakes, dark green forests and then a pock-marked lunar landscape, and was gripped by a vivid memory of the last time he had seen Berlin from the air.

He had been on his twenty-fifth mission as a B-17 pilot, the one mission too many. Remembering a sky treacherous with red flak, Messerschmitt jets stabbing past, planes on either side of his breaking up and dropping slowly downward like falling leaves, he was revisited by that choking fear that had almost paralysed him on what had turned out to be his last mission. But as the Constellation touched down easily and rolled along the runway, the memory of fear dissolved, and he felt only a pleasant tingle of hope and excitement.

Entering another country meant more than customs officers, a passport stamp, and signs in a foreign language. It could mean a new beginning—release from the rut and routine of normal existence, a new life that might turn out to be as disappointing as the old, but at the very least would be so in a different way.

The huge plane shuddered to a stop and he unfastened his seat belt with a sense of release. Well, here you are, back in Berlin, he thought, only this time under very different

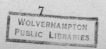

circumstances; now you're a civilian—supposedly a Department of the Air Force employee, Grade GS-15.

He passed through customs quickly, his manner and passport evidence that he was just another routine, harmless government worker, and within half an hour he had taxied to the Harnack House in the quiet American residential quarter of Dahlem. The German desk clerk warmly welcomed him to West Berlin and studied his travel orders for what seemed to Sterling an unnaturally long time before escorting him personally to a VIP suite.

Sterling unpacked, showered, and then went downstairs to the Bavarian Room, where he had two very good martinis and one very bad steak. As he slowly sipped his coffee, killing time until he could start to carry out his instructions and meet his contact, his attention was caught by a young Air Force lieutenant and a very attractive, attentive nurse seated across from him. Both of them were probably in grammar school when he was a lieutenant in the Air Force. For the first time in his life, he was depressed by the feeling that he was getting old, and he was glad when eight o'clock came and he could get out of there.

With a copy of the Paris Edition of the *Herald Tribune* in his right hand and an uncharacteristic green bow tie at his throat, he strolled out of a side door in what he hoped was an inconspicuous manner. Glancing over his shoulder to make certain that he was not being followed, he turned left down a wide, tree-lined avenue flanked by silent, unscarred villas that brooded in the dark sultry night like mausoleums. The outlying suburb of Dahlem at night hadn't changed much since the last time he had seen it, in the spring of 1945; it was still a ghost town devoid of pedestrians, lighted windows, or traffic.

Sterling was a lean, dark man, perhaps an inch over six feet, with frank blue eyes, a touch of white creeping along his thirty-six-year-old temples, and the sort of standard American good looks that weren't likely to attract undue attention. However, as he walked along in the dark, he felt faintly apprehensive—he still wasn't used to the idea that he was now a member of an espionage organization; he had performed quite a few odd jobs in his life, but this was his first attempt at being a spy. And spies, he had read, sometimes got into trouble on dark deserted streets.

But spy, he thought, was too strong a word, the product of a vivid imagination, one of his lesser faults. He reminded himself that he was still an aircraft engineer, on a leave of absence from a five-figure job near Pasadena, and he had been sent to Berlin simply to interrogate a German aircraft engineer who had recently returned to Dresden from the Junkers-B.M.W. Collective at Kuibyshev on the Volga River. That was his only concern—how the agents of the Secret Intelligence Network expected to get this Doctor Eitelfritz Winter out of Dresden would be their problem, not his; in fact, the man who had recruited him had stressed that Sterling's own temporary involvement with high-level espionage would be less dangerous than driving home on Hollywood Freeway at five in the afternoon.

Even now, the memory of that unfortunate analogy caused him a sharp twinge of bitterness. But then, of course, the brisk, well-meaning stranger had briefly forgotten, as so many others had forgotten, that Sterling's wife of eleven years had been killed on the Freeway six months before— probably the real reason for Sterling's quick, eager acceptance of his offer.

Now he was here on this lonely Berlin street, engaging in the unfamiliar business of meeting a contact, because he either had to have a change of air, or suffocate. He had reached the point where he couldn't spend another night alone in the house on Orange Grove Avenue, where the warm glow of love had been replaced by an icy emptiness, nor could he go through another day of meaningless motions at his job.

This was doubly alarming because he had always con-condered it a good, interesting job and he knew he was doing well. But, since his wife's death, the job had suddenly turned stale and flat; it had become confining, sedentary, a well-paid rut. Intelligence work in a foreign country, he hoped, at least would not be that, whatever else it might be.

A sudden whirring noise startled him into wheeling around; he saw a Volkswagen nosing toward him. An ordinary sight, normally, but in the empty dark street the little car, approaching him very slowly with its lights dim, had the sinister air of a monstrous black beetle. But it passed him and Sterling noted with relief the green and yellow United States Army plates beneath the grinning Congo mask of its back.

He walked on and saw a muscular young man with crewcut blond hair standing on a deserted corner. He was dressed in a slope-shouldered cord suit, button-down Oxford shirt, and scuffed white buckskin shoes; he wore a green bow tie and carried in his left hand the Paris Edition of the *Herald Tribune*.

As Sterling passed him, the man said casually, "Excuse me. Do you have a light?"

Sterling stopped and spun the wheel of his Zippo. "Thanks," the man said. "Glad you got here all right. Stay put tonight. Check out at noon tomorrow and meet me in the snack bar of the Truman Hall PX." Then he was off, trailing cigar smoke.

That was easy enough, Sterling thought; now what? He did not feel like returning to the loneliness of his hotel this early, and decided to continue his stroll. There could be no harm in this, he supposed, and a brisk walk might take the edge off his tenseness. He walked for half an hour before being hit by the delayed effect of sleeping fitfully on the plane, but when he turned back in search of the Harnack House and bed, he realized that he was lost, stranded on a wide shadowy avenue lined with bomb-gutted apartment blocks, across from which loomed the dark pines of Grune-wald Forest.

Twenty yards in front of him, he saw a woman approaching a bus stop; although it was a warm June night, she wore a fur coat that hung to her ankles. Odd, he thought, but strolled up and asked her politely in German if she could direct him to the Harnack House.

"Turn around, go straight up Argentinische Allee, cross Kronprinzen Allee—I mean Clay Allee—go up three blocks to Ihnestrasse," the woman replied in cold, staccato English. Then, suddenly, she smiled at him warmly, revealing a gold tooth in the centre of a mouth scarlet with badly applied lipstick. In the orange light of a streetlamp, Sterling saw that she was hardly more than sixteen, plump, and underneath a thick layer of pancake make-up and rouge, pretty in an earthy way. He thanked her and began to leave.

"You in a hurry?" the girl said. Again the gold tooth gleamed.

"Pardon?"

"You in some kind of hurry, I said."

"Well, I have to get back to my hotel."

"You're stayin' at duh Harnack House, huh? You really wanna go back dere, sleep by yerself? Dat's no fun. Gimmee one cigarette."

"I don't have any with me."

"I got some at my place. I got a lot of tings at my place." The girl winked at him invitingly; the gold tooth gleamed.

But nothing that I'm interested in, Sterling thought. Why, he wondered, of all people to ask for directions, did

11

he had to select a streetwalker? But then, he hadn't had much choice. He turned to leave, but the girl reached out and seized his left arm. With a deft movement, she flung apart her coat of dark rabbit fur. Sterling, with one widening left blue eye, saw that she wore nothing beneath the coat, except for two tiny crosses on the tips of her large breasts and black net stockings held up by rubber bands. The effect on him was not so much erotic, as startling, ludicrous.

"You like some of dis, sir?" the girl wheedled, running her pudgy hands over her breasts and down her sturdy thighs, her childish face disfigured by an entreating leer. "Oney ten marks. Or two dollars scrip. Come on. I got a Volkswagen up duh street. We go to my place and I give you fig-fig good."

This is getting ridiculous, Sterling thought, trying to shake loose from the girl's grip.

"We can go over to duh bushes, if you no wanna go to my place," the girl persisted. "Oney ten marks. Nice lookin' man like you, I give you extra good job." She rubbed against him, locking her hands behind his back.

This isn't funny any more, Sterling thought; even in 1945 they weren't this persistent. As a sudden urge of idiot lust hit him, he managed to wrench free and stride off down the street, pursued by the girl's angry shouts: "Whatsa matter, man? You a queer? What you come up to me for, anyhow? Go home and play wid yerself!"

Sterling pressed on, head down, only to bump into a man—no, two men—who suddenly appeared out of the night. One of them was young and resembled an evil dwarf, with his short legs supporting enormous shoulders and long, ape-like arms. He had curly red hair growing low on his forehead, large projecting ears, and wore leather shorts and an Eisenhower jacket with the sleeves cut off. Through his

12

malicious grin floated short, explosive puffs of alcohol fumes.

His companion was a thin handsome man of a rather seedy elegance; he was about Sterling's age but taller, with pale-blond, wavy hair set in a pompadour and a long narrow face. He wore a shabby but well-cut white linen suit and carried a rolled umbrella and an expensive raincoat over his arm; he looked to Sterling like the headwaiter of a three-star restaurant, temporarily unemployed, and mad at the world because of it.

"Why don't you watch where you're going?" he asked sharply.

"Sorry," Sterling said, trying to step between the two men. He wasn't sorry, but he wanted to get out of there.

"'Ere, that won't do," the tall man said. The space closed. "You bloody Yanks think you own the bloody streets?"

Now how did he know that I'm an American, Sterling thought; is it that obvious? "This street is pretty wide," he said, with rising annoyance. "Maybe if you'd kept on your side of it. . . ."

"Well, ain't you the proper mugg?" the tall man asked, tapping the metal tip of his umbrella on the sidewalk. "I've got 'alf a mind to give you a good 'iding."

High heels clattered on the pavement, as the girl ran up to join the two men. "He insulted me. Wanted me to go over into duh bushes wid him. I was waitin' for a bus and he come up and insulted me."

"Insulted the lady, did you?" the tall man said. "Typical of you bloody Yanks. Think you can come over 'ere and treat our German girls like bloody 'ores. Come over into the field and I'll give you what for."

Really angry now, Sterling took a step forward, then checked himself as the thought came to him that he had

13

been ordered to behave inconspicuously; he was no longer free to do as he liked. And then he was further restrained by the weird and suspicious quality of the trio confronting him: the tall man with his cockney phrases delivered with an unmistakable guttural intonation; the dwarfish young man grinning silently, his right hand searching the pocket of his leather shorts; the girl, glaring at him with righteous indignation, taking from her purse a long nail file; all three of them starting to advance on him slowly through the feeble orange light cast by the streetlamp.

"Now let's not do anything really foolish," Sterling said. "Why don't you all just get to hell out of here. . . ."

The girl cackled scornfully. "He's afraid. Schlag his friggin head off."

" 'E is a proper coward now, ain't 'e?" the tall man said, smiling. "Won't even come over into the woods and 'ave it out like a man. Bloody Yank deserves a good 'iding."

"Let's knock that off right now. . . ." Sterling's words were cut off by the dwarfish young man's fist, encased in brass knuckles, shooting toward his jaw. Fortunately, his attacker was so short that Sterling was able to feint away, take the blow on his shoulder, and send him to one knee with a short judo chop, only to be whipped over the back by the tall man's umbrella. Hurt and enraged, no longer in a mood for caution, Sterling scrambled to his feet and lunged at the tall man, bracing himself for the next blow from the umbrella.

It never came. There was some confused shouting in German and English and the two men ran off down the street; Sterling found himself ringed by four large and grinning Negro soldiers.

"Good thing we come along," one of the soldiers, a corporal, chortled. "They was fixin' to lean on you good. What they mad at you for, anyhow?"

14

"I wish I knew," Sterling said. Far off, down the shadowy street, he saw the two men jump into a Volkswagen; it ground into gear and vanished with a squeal of tyres. His mind stirred with vague suspicions. But then he told himself that his imagination was working overtime again. Hadn't his cover been carefully planned, and wasn't the girl, the cause of it all, still there, standing with a sulky expression between two of the soldiers? He drew the corporal aside. "Who's that girl? Ever seen her before?"

"Think I've seen her workin' this street before. Just a little ole *Ami-Hure*. Lots of 'em here this time of night, waitin' for the guys to come out of Club '48."

"And the men?"

"Never seen them two cats before. Drunks most likely, comin' home from that *Gasthaus* round the corner. Or pimps maybe, lookin' to roll you over in the field."

"I see," Sterling said. Although his back ached dully, he felt a surge of relief. "Well, I guess the smartest thing for me to do is to get back to my hotel. Thanks for the helping hand." He wished he could tell his huge benefactor just how thankful he really was, and why, but as a member of the Secret Intelligence Network, he knew that he could not. Regretting this, he wondered if he were really cut out for a life of strict secrecy.

"Max nix," the corporal grinned. "Just don't go wander-in' around here alone again. Berlin may look peaceful, but it ain't. You want some poon, go down the Kudamm. It's safer. But what's a feller like you got to buy it for in this town anyway?"

Sterling smiled at this, and, as though to snuff out the last of his flickering suspicions, to underscore that the girl was nothing more than a harmless streetwalker, and the recent imbroglio just a coincidence, two of the soldiers, after

15

some spirited haggling, headed across the street and into the woods with her.

Sterling strode with quick, lanky strides back to the Harnack House, stopped off at its noisy, crowded bar for a bourbon and soda, and went up to his empty room. He got into bed, but as usual couldn't sleep in the silent dark. He wondered why, with his wife dead for six months now, he still couldn't get used to the idea of her not being there next to him. God knows, during the eleven years they had been together, he had never thought he'd miss her this much.

He got up and flicked on the light, but the sight of the impersonal, white-walled hotel room only increased his feeling of loneliness. He opened his suitcase, took from it a hip flask and swallowed a generous slug of bourbon. Of the three consolations open to a man in his situation, he thought—religion, sex, and alcohol—he had so far tried only the latter. But this time, when he got back into bed, the stinging warmth of the bourbon failed to induce sleep; he still felt restless, tense, bored.

He wondered with alarm if there were anything seriously wrong with him, then reminded himself that he had passed both the lie-detector test and the complete psychiatric examination which the Secret Intelligence Network gave to all its prospective employees. No, he decided, there wasn't anything wrong with him that a change of routine and scenery wouldn't eventually cure.

He longed for the morning to come so he could start thinking about S.I.N.'s problems instead of his own. He wondered if he should mention the street corner hassle to the people at S.I.N. next day, but decided against it. No harm had been done, and he had no greater desire than the next man to admit that he had behaved in public like a damned fool. He did not know anything about espionage but he was certain that a member of the nation's top intelligence organization was not supposed to become involved in a pointless street brawl within hours after arriving at his first overseas station.

But as he lay in the dark thinking, he became less certain of his decision. The two men, he recalled, had driven off in a black Volkswagen. Surely there must be hundreds of black Volkswagens in Berlin, and it had been too far away to notice if it had the same green and yellow plates as the car that had nosed past him earlier, but the more he thought about it, the more he found the coincidence odd, and a little disquieting. It had been eight years since he had been a target for violence, but the memory of it was still there. Hating himself for being unable to control it, he felt the old sensation; anxiety, and then a breath of fear stirring his skin.

2

STERLING WAS met in the PX next afternoon by the same man he had seen on the street corner the night before.

"You're Irving Hodesblatt?" Sterling asked, as they drove off in a black Opel Kapitän with black-and-white KB (West Berlin) plates.

"No. I'm Brooks Twining. Hodesblatt couldn't make it."

Twining offered no further explanation. He drove down Clay Allee, into Grunewald Forest, and down a long narrow dirt road to an isolated villa on the banks of the lake of Grosser Wannsee.

The huge villa, Berlin Base of the organization described in the East German press as a "band of gangsters, saboteurs, wreckers, imperialist hirelings, certified killers, and enemies of the people," was hidden from the road and surrounded by the tall pine trees; upon closer inspection, one could see barbed wire strung between the trees and armed guards patrolling behind the barbed wire. But closer inspection was not encouraged by the signs reading:

ENTRANCE FORBIDDEN TO UNAUTHORIZED
   PERSONNEL
EINTRITT FÜR ZIVIL VERBOTEN
DÉFENSE D'ENTRER
HERUMSTEHEN STRENGSTENS VERBOTEN
U.S. ARMY AMMUNITION SUPPLY DEPOT !
   KEEP OUT !

Sterling was escorted directly to the Office of the Chief of Berlin Base, Harry Chute, a big, broad-boned man in his late fifties with a thatch of iron-grey hair and a soaring forehead, dressed in a wash-and-wear suit that looked as though he had washed it himself, hurriedly. Sterling took an instant liking to Chute, who, he had heard, had been a successful corporation lawyer, and, during the war, the director of a famous network in Berne that had reached into the experimental rocket laboratories at Peenemünde. Now he had once again left his law practice to assume direction of Berlin Base, although officially he was represented as a State Department minister dealing with east-west trade problems. Sterling wondered idly if anyone who really counted was deceived by that.

"Glad to have you aboard, Sterling. Pete, isn't it?" Chute said, shaking hands. "Any trouble on the trip over?"

Sterling said that the trip had been uneventful, paused, and added that his first evening in Berlin had not.

Chute listened with patient interest until he had finished, then said, in a wry tone that gave Sterling the uncomfortable feeling that he was being considered more than a little naïve, "We'll make a note of that, of course. We make a note of everything, can't afford not to. But I think I can assure you that the other side had nothing to do with it. But do us both a favour and don't go wandering around the streets again alone and at night. Now let's get down to the business at hand."

Chute leafed through a dossier stamped *Top Secret, Eyes Only*, lit a pipe and said, "You've been brought over here to interrogate one Doctor Eitelfritz Winter, presently residing at Rankestrasse 23, Dresden, DDR, just back after eight years at Kuibyshev. Winter had the misfortune to be one of

19

those German scientists rounded up in Operation Osaviak-him in 1945 and sent to work in the Soviet Union. Naturally we wanted him for Paperclip, but somebody goofed. Now that he's back, we, and especially the Air Force, think he can tell us a lot about those MIG's that raised such hell in Korea and possibly a lot more about a new Soviet bomber with a twelve-thousand-hp turbo-prop engine that's better than anything we have on the drawing board. It's an important operation, and one that we think we can pull off. Now Washington has told me that you're a damned fine aircraft engineer, but Winter, from the evidence of his work with jet engines for Junkers during the war, is something of a genius. If we get him, do you think you can handle him?"

"If I can't," Sterling said, "you can always send him back to the States for further interrogation."

Chute took the pipe stem from his mouth and scratched his jaw with it. "That's unfortunately not practicable. Winter was a Nazi. Purely a nominal Party Member, of course, but under the present immigration laws, he's barred from the States. We can get around the law in special cases, but we don't like to do it unless it becomes unavoidable. The job should be done over here."

"If you can produce Winter, I'm pretty sure I can find out what he knows."

"Fair enough," Chute said. "Why don't we get on with it then, and introduce you to your case officer?"

"I'd expected to meet him before this," Sterling said. "They told me in Washington that Irving Hodesblatt was one of your best men."

"Hodesblatt?" Chute examined the bowl of his pipe. "Why, Irv isn't responsible for this case any more. He flew home yesterday. I guess they got my cable on it after you left."

Sterling waited for a fuller explanation of a development which sounded highly unusual to him. He was a little annoyed when Chute gave none, but only pressed a buzzer and began to refill his pipe. Within two minutes a man appeared who was introduced to Sterling as Ray Duffy.

His right hand tingling from the crush of Duffy's hand-shake, Sterling observed him and decided that he was the first Secret Intelligence Network employee he had met who looked the part of a secret agent. He was one of those people whose age is difficult to judge, for his physique—six feet tall, lean, muscular—was that of a college athlete, while his drawn, starkly handsome features were those of an ageing adventurer who has survived (narrowly, one suspected) odd and dangerous experiences in strange places.

Duffy's lined and leathery face, split by a long, straight, sword-like nose, was as bronze and impassive as that of an Indian, and contrasted in a rather startling way with his light-blond hair and electric-blue eyes which regarded the world stoically from beneath thin white eyebrows. He spoke in guarded, subdued tones, and yet looked capable of sudden violence. Ray Duffy, Sterling decided, was not the sort of man one would creep up behind and slap on the back when he wasn't looking.

"First thing I want you to do with friend Sterling, Ray," Chute said, "is to get him a decent billet."

"He could move into Hodesblatt's place. It's a nice house, all furnished, and Irv left the keys with me."

"Good idea. Why not take care of it right now?" Chute stood up and shook Sterling's hand with a hearty grip that inspired confidence. "It's been nice talking to you, Sterling. One last thing. I'm responsible for scores of other operations working out of this base, so I can't give this one my personal attention. I hope you'll understand when I say that nothing could make me happier than not seeing either

21

of you two again until Ray here tells me he has Doctor Winter ready for your interrogation."

"No reason why you should, Harry," Duffy said, with quiet confidence. "We'll handle it from here."

He led Sterling out of the Chief's office, took him on a tour of the Berlin Base without introducing him to any of its personnel, and then said, "To protect your cover, we'll have to drive over to Clay Allee now and let Berlin Military Post process you just as though you were a newly arrived D.A.F. civilian. You'll also have to do some consulting work for the Air Force, just to keep up appearances. The C.O. knows about you, so a few hours a week and a few reports should make you look legitimate."

After Sterling had completed his processing and paid a token visit to Tempelhof, Duffy said, "Almost six-thirty. You must be getting hungry. How about having dinner with me?"

"You don't have to go to all that trouble."

"No trouble. You can't have dinner in your billet, since you don't have a housekeeper, and I won't let you eat that swill the Harnack House serves up. I'll see about getting you a good housekeeper with security clearance in the morning."

They drove to the Swedish Pavilion on the banks of Grosser Wannsee and dined on Rhine wine and salted pig's knuckles at a table in a deserted corner. Duffy chatted pleasantly about this and that, but diplomatically turned aside Sterling's efforts to bring Winter into the conversation. The polite caginess he had so far encountered at S.I.N. started to get on Sterling's nerves, and, as they drove back toward Dahlem, he said, "Last time I looked at a map, Dresden was a hundred miles south of Berlin. Our friend must be guarded constantly. It's probably none of my business, but I'd like to know just how you people expect to get him out of there so I can talk to him."

"That's right, it is none of your business. At least not yet," Duffy said, pulling up before a house in the plush section of the Dahlem suburb. "Well, here it is, your new home. It's one of the best in town. Irv was a man who knew how to live."

"It's still assigned to Hodesblatt, then?" Sterling said. "Does that mean he's coming back to Berlin?"

"Maybe, but not until after you've gone."

"You don't think he'll mind my staying here?"

"How can he mind? It's a requisitioned billet, doesn't belong to him."

The house was pure 1928 Bauhaus in style and would provide quite a home away from home, Sterling thought. It looked like a grey concrete pillbox decorated with enormous plate-glass windows. A high hedge shielded it from adjacent villas and Hindenburgstrasse, which was as dark and lifeless as the boardwalk of a beach resort on a winter evening.

Duffy helped him carry his bags to the door, then said, "Here are the keys. I've still got a few contacts to see tonight, so I won't go in and show you around. Twining will be over to pick you up in the morning."

Sterling thanked him for the dinner, said goodnight, and entered the vast silent house, whose interior decoration proved to be, not Bauhaus, but Grand Rapids. Here and there among the impersonal pieces of Quartermaster furniture, however, could be noted traces of the recently departed tenant's personality: a wellstocked portable bar, Lithographs by Marc Chagall and chaim Soutine, scores of books on the occult sciences, a pink plastic ash tray in the shape of a life-sized human hand. The latter clutched a dead cigar butt.

Sterling, hearing the steady plop-plop of a leaky faucet, walked into the kitchen; the lights didn't work. He examined the living room windows; they were all open to the dark humid night. He picked up the phone; it was dead. He found himself wishing that he were back in the Harnack House, or that Hodesblatt were still around. But he checked this line of thought; S.I.N. must know what it was doing in billeting him in this isolated spot. However, just for the hell of it, he opened one of his bags, took from its lining his one war souvenir, an engraved Walther Mark II PPK, loaded it, and slipped it into his pocket.

He carried his bags upstairs to the doorway of what he judged to be the master bedroom, felt for the light switch and located it just as he heard the faint, but unmistakable sound of human breathing in the darkness. His old training conquering his sudden chilling alarm, he flicked on the light, dropped to his knees and whipped out the pistol.

Lying on an immense, non-Quartermaster Issue double bed directly in front of him was a human figure. It was that of a young girl. She was sleeping on her right side, clutching a pillow to her bosom and, on this warm night, she was not wearing any clothes. In the garish light of a bare light bulb, her buttocks had the symmetry and colour of half moons.

The girl moaned, released the pillow, writhed about, and came to rest on her back. The almond-coloured tips of her breasts regarded Sterling accusingly. She was very beautiful and couldn't have been more than twenty. She had long, jet-black hair. Across her firm belly ran an appendicitis scar.

Sterling's immediate reaction was one of immense relief; then, in quick succession, he felt a little foolish (he wouldn't tell Chute about this), excited by the strange naked girl, and baffled as to what she was doing here or what he was

24

supposed to do about it. He couldn't stand there gawking at her, pleasant as he found this to be, and he couldn't leave; this was, after all, his house. Recovering from his first eye-bugging astonishment, he picked up one of his suitcases, dropped it to the floor, and gave an exaggerated cough.

This had no effect, except to make the sleeping girl move her long, well-shaped legs. A charming smile, as at some remembered pleasure, curled her full lips. Sterling picked up two suitcases and dropped them to the floor.

This worked. The girl jerked up; when she caught sight of the tall silent figure framed in the shadowy doorway, her green eyes widened in astonishment and fright. Sterling was thankful that she did not scream, but only armoured herself in bedsheets and demanded, in a strong Berlin accent, *"Mensch, ver sind sie dann? Was wollen sie dann von mir?"*

Sterling, a man who had lived with fear, knew how to recognize its face and when he saw that the girl, for all her attempts at bravado, was genuinely terrified, he smiled and said quickly, "I'm the new tenant of this billet. It was assigned to me this afternoon by Berlin Military Post."

"Oh," she said. "Oh." Relief warmed her face, but she made no effort to explain her presence, only staring at Sterling as though he were a friendly Martian.

"That's who I am," he said. "Now I think I ought to ask you who you are."

"My name is Christiane Stock. I'm Mr. Hodesblatt's housekeeper."

Housekeeper, Sterling thought. It was hard to picture her toiling with mop and frying pan, but then this was Berlin. "Well, Fräulein Stock," he said, "suppose I just wait down-stairs while you get dressed. There are a few things I think we ought to discuss."

Fräulein Stock joined him in five minutes in the living

room, dressed in flat shoes and a sack-like, faded grey house dress, which effectively disguised a fact of which Sterling was already aware; that she had the finest figure he had ever seen on a woman, and he had seen more than a few.

Before he could speak, Fräulein Stock launched into rapid-fire English, "I've been Mr. Hodesblatt's housekeeper for three months. He used to have an old woman, but he caught her stealing his coffee and had to fire her. When he had to go back home in a hurry, he gave me money to keep his place clean and stop burglars from breaking in. There are a lot of burglars in the American sector. But he didn't tell me that anyone else would be staying here while he was gone. Mr. Hodesblatt—"

"Then you're the official housekeeper assigned by Berlin Military Post to this billet?"

"Yes, sir. Mr. Hodesblatt—"

"Do you have any proof of that?"

"Of course, sir." Formidable *Ausweise,* from both B.M.P. and the Labour Office of the City of West Berlin, were produced; they looked genuine.

"Mr. Hodesblatt was very satisfied with my work, sir," the girl went on. "I hope you'll let me stay. I could work for you until Mr. Hodesblatt returns."

Now that, thought Sterling, would not be at all hard to take, but he said nothing.

"Please, sir," the girl persisted. "I really need this job. It's hard to get a job in Berlin."

"It's all kinds of irregular," Sterling hedged. "I'm not at all sure that I'm in a position. . . ."

"Please, sir. Why don't you talk to Mr. Duffy, Mr. Hodesblatt's friend? He knows me. He'll tell you that I'm a very good cook and housekeeper."

The girl looked so genuinely concerned that Sterling said, "I guess I can do that much. I'll speak to Duffy in the morning. If he, or B.M.P., has no objection, maybe we can work something out."

"Thanks a lot, sir. I'm sure that it will be all right. You'll need a housekeeper, anyway."

"Don't count on anything. The final decision won't be up to me."

"It will be all right. You'll see." She rose and headed for the staircase, as though the matter had been settled.

"Where are you going to now, Fräulein Stock?"

"Upstairs, sir. To straighten up your room and make your bed. I'm sorry I slept in it, but I thought I would be alone, and my room is small and hot."

"You live here, too, then?"

"Yes, sir. I have the maid's room in the attic."

"You live here all the time?"

"Yes, sir. Just like all the housekeepers."

"I see. Well, goodnight then Fräulein Stock."

She nodded, started to mount the stairs, then paused.

"Excuse me, sir, but could you tell me if you are married?"

Sterling immediately felt the old twinge of bitterness. "Why do you ask that?"

"Well, most of the gentlemen who are assigned to these large houses are married. If you are expecting your wife from the States, I would have to plan—"

"I'm not expecting her from the States. She's dead—" Sterling checked himself, and felt ashamed. He really had to control this impulse to lash out at people who could not know what they were saying. "You'll just have me to contend with," he added, in a calmer tone.

"I'm sorry," the girl said. She walked up a few more steps, then paused again. "I hope you won't mind my saying this, sir, but I'm glad you are staying here tonight."

He looked at her, searching for some invitation behind what struck him as a curious remark, but saw that her face

27

was expressionless. She was the reserved, deferential house-keeper, only fantastically prettier than most. He wished he could think of something light and witty to say, to the effect that he was not exactly sorry that she was staying here, either, but he had never been very good at badinage. All he could think of was, "Really? Why?"

"You remember what I said about burglars?" she said. "Well, when I came home from the movies an hour ago, I saw two strange men standing in the garden. I was so frightened that I could hardly run to the phone to call the M.P.'s, but the phone was turned off—"

"Two men! What did they look like?"

"I don't know, sir. I was so frightened, and it was so dark—"

"Was one tall, the other short, like a dwarf?"

"I don't know, sir. But it turned out all right. When they saw the lights going on, they just walked away, got into their car and drove off."

"Car? What kind of car?"

"I think it was a Volkswagen, sir."

"What colour?"

"Black, I think. But there's nothing to worry about. They were probably Americans, visiting their girl friends in one of the neighbouring houses. You see, as they drove away, I saw that their car had the green and yellow United States Army plates."

3

STERLING SPENT a sleepless night, unnecessarily as it turned out, with the Walther next to him on his night table and his door locked. The first thing he did when he saw Ray Duffy next morning was to tell him about the two men in the garden.

Duffy steepled his fingers, gazed thoughtfully through the iron bars of his single window at the tall pines of Grunewald, then looked back at Sterling with the hint of a smile in his eyes. "So you think the Russians have sent two characters over here to murder you," he said. "You've only been here two nights and you're beginning to think along lines like that."

"I don't know what to think," Sterling said. "I'm just telling you it seems damned strange to me."

"You can't be a paranoid, or they wouldn't have selected you for this assignment."

"What?"

"I mean, it's not possible that you have delusions of persecution, imagine people are following you, plotting against you?"

"Of course not," Sterling said. He was getting angry.

"Just thought I'd ask. You must have a lively imagination, at least. Let me explain this a little more thoroughly than Harry had time to. First, it's impossible that your cover could have been penetrated this quickly. Second, the M.V.D. and the S.S.D—that's the East German secret

29

police, don't come over into West Berlin putting the arm on our people. They just don't. Behind the iron curtain, of course, it's a different story. And try to understand this. If they were behind this, wouldn't it be an obvious tip-off that they knew we were after Winter? Now, they're not as efficient as they're cracked up to be, but they're not dumb, either. They work very, very quietly. This whole business is just coincidence. There must be fifty black Volkswagens in the B.M.P. Motor Pool alone."

Duffy spoke with such a mixture of authority and amused tolerance that Sterling, again feeling that he had been a little naïve, decided to drop the subject once and for all. He was new to Berlin and a novice at this trade, while Duffy had been operating there for years as a professional espionage agent and should know what he was talking about. But when Sterling mentioned Christiane, Duffy's unconcerned manner suddenly vanished.

"Balls!" he said in an agitated voice, sitting up in his chair. "I forgot all about her."

"You know her? She really is a housekeeper?"

"What? Oh, sure, she's a housekeeper. But I never thought Irv would ask her to watch his house while he's away. Now we have a problem."

"But one that can be solved easily enough. I'll tell her I have another housekeeper."

"You can't do that. It might make her suspicious. Besides, she's harmless."

"She doesn't look like any housekeeper I've ever seen."

"You'll see a lot of things in Berlin you've never seen before. What does she look like to you?"

"Like a very attractive girl who was probably sleeping with Hodesblatt after she finished ironing his shirts."

Duffy eyed Sterling coldly for a few seconds, then grinned. "You're right on the first count and probably right on the second. Irv was a bachelor. A moody, lonely guy, and his work made him more so. He found this Christiane waiting table in some crummy *Kneipe* in Wedding, felt sorry for her, and took her in. She's got a mother and father living in the East Sector and since this gives her a legitimate reason to cross the sector borders, Irv was planning to develop her as a courier. He did manage to finagle a clearance for her as a maid, but he never got around to the courier bit. She's a good worker, oddly enough. But I wish he'd said something to me about having her stay in the house. Guess he left in too much of a hurry. It's the only mistake I've ever known him to make. He worked on this Winter thing for four years and really set it up beautifully. But let's forget him and Christiane. Poor Irv. . . ."

Duffy shook his head, studied some papers on his desk, looked up suddenly and said, "Pete, I have a proposition for you. It's strictly my own idea. When you agreed to take on this temporary assignment, I know that you did so on the understanding that you would be responsible only for the technical interrogation. Right?"

"That's right."

"Well, Irv's leaving has changed the situation a bit. I backstopped him on this, but now I don't have anyone to backstop me. We're always short-handed here. I really could use a little help with the contacts and agents, and you can speak German, probably better than I can. Now you don't have to get involved with this if you don't want to. But frankly, it could get a little dull for you just sitting around waiting for Winter to turn up. I'm not trying to pressure you into anything, though. If you don't want any part of operational work, and most of our temporary experts don't, we can forget my proposition and no hard feelings."

"I'd be glad to help in any way I can. But you better start telling me more about Winter than you have up to now."

"He's already accepted our offer. One of Irv's top agents, a Dresden professor and old friend of Winter's, has already contacted him. He sent back word through a cut-out that Winter is not only willing, but eager to talk to us. He has every reason to come West, you see. He owns property in Bavaria and Westphalia. He has money in Swiss banks, which would be hard to touch if he stays in Dresden. He's in line for a really important job in the Ruhr. We're going to pay him thirty thousand dollars in greenbacks. His only living blood relative, a sister, lives here in West Berlin. But the clincher is that he hates the Russians' guts."

"That can't be too unusual."

"It is, though. The other five engineers who returned with him seem contented enough. If they play ball with the government, they get inflated salaries, free cars and houses, unlimited research facilities, the works. But nothing could hold Winter any place where the Russians are in control. He was in Berlin when the Mongolians came in in 1945, and some nasty things happened to his wife. Anyway, she died. Then when they grabbed him in the middle of the night and sent him to Kuibyshev, the plane he was on was forced to fly above the clouds to avoid a storm. There wasn't any oxygen equipment available for the passengers and Winter damn near suffocated. He did his work at Kuibyshev, but he was always causing trouble in little ways. At one official party celebrating the end of the Great Fatherland War, he appeared half crocked and wearing a tightly-knotted rope for a tie. Only the fact that he was so damned valuable saved him from real trouble on that one."

"How do you know all this?"

"We have our sources."

"All right, he wants to defect. Dresden is still a hundred miles inside the Soviet Zone."

Duffy grinned. "We're not going to kidnap Winter, hide him in a barrel, or spirit him off through the woods at midnight disguised as a charwoman. Forget all that comic book stuff. We work along rational lines here. Winter, you see, is coming to East Berlin to attend a big scientific conference at Humboldt University. We'll make our move to bring him out then."

"But won't he be watched constantly?"

"Of course they'll watch him. But they can't watch him all the time. They can't put a ball and chain on him, crawl into bed with him, or go to the john with him. Keep in mind that Winter is a very important and valuable man to the East German government. They need high-level scientific help desperately. They can't afford to treat him like some poor Schlub. They have to maintain the illusion that he loves them, too—give him elbow room. When they do, one of our agents will bring him out. And here is something else you ought to understand. Despite what you may have read, despite what you may have heard, there is still no real restriction on free passage between East and West Berlin. With Stalin dead, that's truer than ever. Entry into the East Zone is something else again. It's sealed off tighter than a cod piece. You need papers, and there are armed guards, road blocks, ditches, barbed wire along every inch of the zonal borders. But there is still absolutely nothing to prevent an East Berliner from simply walking down Unter den Linden, through the Brandenburger-Tor, and into the British Sector. As long as those sector borders are wide open, we have a chance. We're counting on the element of surprise. The Russians might suspect that we want to talk to Winter, but they don't know it for sure, and they certainly don't know how we intend to get him. And once he's over

33

here, they won't come after him. He's too famous for them to try any rough stuff and risk an international incident once he's safely in our hands."

"Who are these agents you're so sure can bring him out?"

"That's not for you to know. I'm not being cagey, Pete. In this business, you're only told exactly what you need to to know to do your own job. It's better all the way around. Better for you, better for S.I.N. If something goes wrong, no one man can blow the whole operation. But I can tell you that we have two active agents and one passive contact. None of the three know each other. Which one we finally use depends on the circumstances at the time. I'm going downtown tonight to pick up a drop from one of them. If you don't want to mix into this, now is your last chance to say so. Let me warn you that the hours are long, and some aspects of the work pretty raunchy."

"I'll go. I want to go."

"Good. Get yourself a car from the motor pool, spend the afternoon at Tempelhof, and I'll pick you up at your place at nine."

"Now that I'm in this with you, how about telling me why Hodesblatt left Berlin."

"I honestly would rather beg off that one, Pete. It's a personal thing and has nothing to do with our handling of Winter. I'll tell you if you insist, but please don't insist."

Sterling did not insist, for, as he watched Duffy locking up the Winter dossier, his attention was diverted by a curious object resting on the top of the safe.

It was a small magneto alternator, to him not unusual in itself, but from it dangled two long thin steel wires whose terminal points were the grasping jaws of tiny steel pincers.

"What the devil is that thing?" Sterling said. The disturbing thought flashed through his mind that this was something S.I.N. used in its work.

"That?" Duffy said. He picked up the wires and fixed one of the toothed clips to Sterling's right wrist, the other to the flesh of his neck. "The S.S.D. over in East Berlin use this in interrogations. One of my subagents got it for me. By turning this knob, you can control the shooting of a terrific electric current through the body. It's a little bit like being in the electric chair, only you don't die right away. It's a big improvement over the rubber truncheons of the Gestapo. Science marches on."

Sterling took off the clips and stared at them with fascinated disgust. Duffy grinned at him. "Don't worry," he said. "They'll never use them on you. We only have foreign nationals doing our undercover work in East Germany. If they're blown, we drop them cold, and nobody can ever hang anything on S.I.N. You see, Pete, you're working for an organization that doesn't exist."

4

STERLING CHECKED a B.M.W. sedan out of the motor pool
and drove all the way to the Airlift Memorial in front of
Tempelhof before deciding that he really did not want to go
through the farce of pretending to be a visiting aircraft consultant this afternoon. Besides, he told himself, as he drove
back toward Hindenburgstrasse, there was something he
really should do.

He let himself into the villa, but Christiane was not there.
Her absence disturbed him. He walked upstairs, looking
for her, but she was neither on the second floor nor in her
own room in the attic, which was, as she had said, small
and hot. It was also, he noted, directly above his and its
walls were hung with cheap reproductions of paintings
by Paul Klee and Joan Miro; not the usual thing for a maid.
He opened her wardrobe and saw with relief the cotton
dresses still hanging there; at least, he thought, she hasn't
left.

He went downstairs and glanced at his wristwatch; five
o'clock, the cocktail hour. He mixed himself a large dry
martini and stretched out on an aluminium chaise-longue in
the back garden. A fine spring rain had just dropped and
he had a view of curving paths and wet flowers, a soggy
hammock swaying in the breeze, two starlings fluttering in
an overflowing bird bath. It should have been a sight to
soothe and quiet the mind, but it did nothing for him.

In a few hours, he thought, he would be getting into

something he had not bargained for : undercover espionage work. The prospect intrigued him, but disturbed him a little, too. Of course he wanted to help, because he knew better than the non-technical people at S.I.N. how valuable Winter really was, and he had come here hoping to see something different, but, remembering the dangling clips of electrodes on Duffy's safe, he was not sure that it had been wise to accept quite so quickly an offer to work in a field for which he was not trained and which might well turn out to be—not exciting—but monotonous, depressingly sinister and dangerous.

It wasn't that he was afraid. Or was it? He could never be sure, he thought. Those last few B-17 missions, when he had lived with the terror of approaching death, had shaken him up more than he had ever admitted to anyone. Perhaps, he thought, his whole way of life since 1945 had been conditioned by that experience. He had chosen to play it safe, and had been more than content with a house in the suburbs, a little tennis and boating, nine to five over the drawing board, two weeks every summer at Lake Tahoe, the years going by as gently and with as little variety as the southern California seasons.

Now, at thirty-six, he suddenly found himself alone; no children, no relatives, no real friends because he had never felt the need for any and had never made the necessary effort. He had always seen himself as a man content to leave other people in peace, and asking nothing more than that they do the same for him, because he found people— especially in groups—disappointing.

He wondered now if that, too, was just an excuse. Perhaps he had avoided close contact with people because he was afraid, afraid that intimacy would lead to trouble, shatter the comfortable little wall he had built around himself. He really ought to try to get with it again, he told himself, but then recalled with a shudder two women in Arcadia, golfing partners of his wife, who had telephoned him not five days after the funeral. . . .

He thought of his job. He had liked it and been interested in it but now he wondered if that, too, had been an excuse, a compromise, the easiest way to pay for the groceries and the good life in a sun-drenched suburb. There had been times when he had considered going into business for himself, into a research lab, or back to the University of California for advanced courses, but each time he had gotten another raise and settled for being a hired-hand—a well-paid one—but a hired-hand nevertheless. He was an expert in the design of turbine engines, but what really intrigued him was missile research, space probes. To switch to these fields, however, would have required a certain amount of sacrifice and he had been unwilling (or afraid, he wondered?) to try something relatively new.

Hell, Sterling, he thought, you're in bad shape, but you're not a bad guy, really, and let's stop giving yourself a hard time. He got up to mix himself another martini when he saw Christiane walking toward the back door leading to the kitchen. She was wearing a cheap raincoat and carrying a lot of packages.

"Hello, there," he said, opening the door for her and helping her with the packages. "I thought you'd like to know that it's all right for you to stay here."

"I knew it would be," she said.

Her reaction surprised him. He had not expected her to display gratitude, but he had thought she would be pleased at the news. Instead she was very cool and matter of fact and more poised than any twenty-year-old girl had a right to be.

"When would you like to have dinner?" she asked.

"Any time. No, that's not quite right. I'm going down-

38

town tonight at nine."

"Then I'd better start it right now. Is there anything you'd like me to make?"

"I'll leave that up to you," he said, thinking: *at least she's stopped calling me sir*. He made himself another martini and returned to the solitude of the garden. Christiane, he thought, was about the same age as his wife when he had married her. But there, the similarity ended. His wife had not been outstandingly attractive in the conventional sense, she had been born in a Spanish-Moorish villa in Fresno, her father had been an executive of the Bank of America, she had gone to Mills College, she had been popular, secure, and successful at everything she had tried except having children. God only knew what this girl's background was, what she had gone through in this chaotic, battered city.

How many thousands of young girls like Christiane must there be in Berlin? He wondered. Girls for whom nothing could be done, who had no hope, whose very attractiveness was a kind of disadvantage, and yet who managed to survive, to retain a little independence, a little spirit. His own problems, he though, would probably seem banal and easily solvable to her.

Dark had begun to settle about the garden when she called him in to dinner. He immediately regretted his quick decision not to tell her what he wanted to eat, for she served him an all too German, or Berlin (there was a difference, he knew) meal: a sour broth thickened with strips of tripe, followed by fat eels cooked in small pieces and smothered in a rich sauce, boiled potatoes, and cucumber salad, the whole formidable mess to be savoured with a mug of Schultheiss beer.

It was by far the strangest meal he had ever eaten, seated alone in this huge spare dining room at a formica table constructed in the shape of a kidney. He had never had a servant, certainly not as a boy growing up on the citrus ranch in Tulare, California, although a cleaning woman had come in twice a week to help his wife those last years in Arcadia. Now he had an attractive girl serving him dinner, moving around him in a thin cotton dress, her figure a study in rounded surfaces, and he felt strange little waves of sensation move along his nerves.

The situation, he thought, was a little ludicrous, but disturbing, too, for as she served him coffee, he was suddenly visited by a vivid mental image of Christiane as he had seen her for the first time; sleeping on her side, naked, in what was now his bed. He saw again that slightly petulant mouth, the green eyes growing round with fright, the long hair cascading over her shoulders, luminously black against the dull white of the bedsheets wrapped around her ripe young body.

Damn, Sterling, he thought, get a grip on yourself; they didn't send you over here for this. But the fact remained that Christiane intrigued him, perhaps because, quite apart from being beautiful, she had said nothing during the entire meal. Whenever strangers tried to engage him in conversation, to get close to him, he knew that he had the tendency to withdraw; he'd been pretty much of a dud at sales conventions. But this girl acted as though he weren't really there; it gave him an odd desire to talk to her. Or was this just because he wanted to talk to another human being, and she was the closest one at hand?

He finished his coffee and went out to the kitchen, where he found her energetically washing the dishes. "Thank you," he said. "That was a very nice dinner."

"I'm glad you liked it," she said, without taking her eyes from the sink. "Most Americans don't like our Berlin cooking."

40

He was trying to think of a suitable reply to that, when she walked out of the kitchen with a pail of garbage. He felt awkward and a little foolish standing there by himself and thought that this girl was a little too reserved to be true. He wondered what she and Hodesblatt had talked about when they weren't sleeping together. But then he wasn't even sure that they had been sleeping together. He wanted to believe that they hadn't, and her room in the attic did give the impression that she lived there, while the departed Hodesblatt, from what little he had heard about him, was an odd sort of fish.

When she returned, he made another attempt. "Mr. Duffy told me that your parents live in East Berlin."

"Yes, but I don't see them very much. East Berlin isn't a very nice place, you know."

Again she returned to the soap suds in the sink, ignoring him. He suddenly had the idea of telling her to forget about the dishes and join him in the living room for a drink, but glanced at his wristwatch and saw that this would not be wise. But he wanted to shake her maddening composure and wondered wryly what her reaction would be if he said, "I'd like very much to talk to you, but unfortunately in ten minutes I have to begin my new career as a spy." Probably no reaction at all; spies must be a common thing in Berlin, like rubble, or uniforms.

He heard a horn blow twice. That would be Duffy; he was the type to be early. Now, he thought, is your last chance to duck out of undercover espionage work; it's not too late, and nobody will hand you a white feather if you do. He hesitated and then went toward the door, impelled more by curiosity than anything else. "I have to go downtown now with Mr. Duffy," he said. "I don't know when I'll be back," he added, and then thought that that was a rather irrelevant thing to say.

"You'll have a good time," she said. "Mr. Hodesblatt and Mr. Duffy were always going out together at night, and they always seemed to have a good time."

He was sure that he detected a note of irony in her voice, but he had no time to explore the reasons for it. He went out the door and toward his temporary new occupation, thinking that he had always considered spies (when he thought about them at all) rather exotic and slightly disreputable. But this was a naïve, unrealistic attitude, he told himself, in this year, 1953, when a spy was no longer a buck-toothed Japanese houseboy, a bearded Balkan with a bomb, or a multi-lingual Greek from Smyrna, but more likely a former classmate, your uncle, or the man seated next to you on the eight-fifteen commuters' special. The resurgence of an ancient trade was just another dreary sign of the times, he thought, and America, no longer able to afford innocence, had to have spies, too, as a form of survival insurance. Therefore, he, Peter Sterling, might as well get into the act; at least he was playing in America's first-time team in the field.

Duffy seemed rather impatient when he got into the Borgward sedan. "Let's mach schnell," he said. "We've got our work cut out for us tonight. Christiane took care of you all right for dinner, I hope?"

"Yes," Sterling said, "although she doesn't have much to say."

"When you look like that, who needs to say anything? And why should she have anything to say? She's just a maid, isn't she?"

Sterling had to admit to himself that Duffy had him there; in Europe, maids didn't talk to their employers except in line of duty. Still. . . .

They drove out of the unscarred suburbs toward Kurfürstendamm and, though this was eight years after the war's

42

end, Sterling soon saw the familiar grotesque skeletons of buildings; the acre after desolate acre of flat empty land; the long, grey, unpeopled streets cutting through deserts of rubble. The passing scene struck him as giving off an uncanny aura of death, uneasiness, a sense of dark things lurking in a twilight world.

"Been here before?" Duffy asked.

"Just for a week, in 'forty-five. I don't really know Berlin," Sterling said, looking out the window. He was beginning to wonder just how much of this dark, dreary wasteland he and his B-17 crew were personally responsible for, when the car crossed Wilmersdorferstrasse and the melancholy ruins gave way abruptly to a long, wide avenue, ablaze with neon and lined on both sides with luxury shops, hotels, night clubs, restaurants, outdoor cafés, movie palaces, and colourful posters announcing the opening of the III. International Berlin Film Festival.

This incongruous oasis of light and gaiety vanished as soon as the car had skirted the shell of the Kaiser Wilhelm Memorial Church; Duffy drove under the S-Bahn Elevated Railway to the shadowy district of Hasenheide, where he swung into the parking lot of the Resi-Ballhaus.

"You're not going to pick up an important message in a place like this?" Sterling said.

"This barn is the ideal place for it," Duffy answered. "Once you start meeting contacts in alleys and abandoned bunkers you'll be burned in no time. Come on, let's go in. Just speak English exclusively and act the part of a Department of the Air Force civilian out for an evening of fun and games."

Sterling had always avoided the frantic, commercial jollity of night clubs, but he was intrigued by the *Resi*. He stared with amused disbelief at its gleaming parquet floor the size of a basketball court, around which were arranged

43

in tiers hundreds of little cubicles with numbered dial telephones and pneumatic tubes, and at the weird spectacle drawing to a close on the stage as they sat down. Fountains of water—emerald, silver, purple, scarlet, gold—rose and fell in front of a velvet curtain, swaying like dancers in time to the *Emperor Waltz*.

"The famous *Resi* Water Ballet," Duffy said. "They shoot water through hidden jets and then colour it with hidden spotlights. Only the Germans could expend so much energy and ingenuity to produce a monstrosity like that."

Sterling glanced around and began to suspect that Duffy was pulling his leg; it was difficult to believe that in this festive mob of ordinary Berlin burghers and Allied soldiers there was a real secret agent, waiting to deliver a message unobserved. "You're kidding," he said.

"You'll see," Duffy said. "Just let me handle it. What do you want to drink?"

"I'm a bourbon man."

"The branch water isn't very good here. Better stick with cognac, we might have a long night ahead of us." Duffy snapped over a waiter in white tie and tails and ordered as the multi-coloured fountains expired to warm applause. In the garish white light that suddenly flooded the crowded room, Stirling noticed that his companion's appearance and manner had undergone a startling transformation.

Until tonight, Duffy had always been neatly and conservatively dressed. He had spoken in quiet, precise tones; his expression, while impassive, had been intelligent; he had rarely smoked, and then only mild Player's cigarettes. Now he was dressed in suede shoes, a pink shirt, an ecru bow tie, and a pale green gabardine suit with immense padded shoulders; he chewed on a foul-smelling, unlit cigar; he grinned constantly and rather foolishly; he leered and winked roguishly at girls at the adjoining rables.

Then he began to drum on the table with his palms and to snap his fingers as a twenty-piece orchestra trooped on to the stage. The white light dimmed to a purplish haze; most of the guests fought toward the dance floor as though jostling into a subway entrance at rush hour; a portly tenor in a tuxedo fondled the microphone and began groan :

"In Honolulu auf der Hafenbar. . . ."

Immediately, the table telephone next to Sterling's head blazed red. Duffy grabbed the receiver, engaged in a few moments of idiotic banter, then handed it over to Sterling. "She wants you Pete."

Sterling placed the receiver against his ear in an attempt to hear clearly over the blasting rhythms of the band. "No, no," he almost shouted into the mouthpiece. "Thanks, but not just now. I'm not very good at the polka, you see. Yes, yes, danke, goodbye." He replaced the telephone on its hook. "What the hell was that, Ray?"

"Somebody ask you to dance?"

"Insisted is more like it."

"That's what the table telephones are for. If you see someone you like, you phone and ask her to dance or join you for a drink. Or, if you prefer, you can make your pitch via the pneumatic tube. That's the big attraction of this barn."

Three more telephoned invitations to the dance followed in quick succession; all for Sterling; all refused.

"Listen, Pete," Duffy whispered, "you'd better accept the next call or it will look odd. We came here to ball, remember?"

"Why don't *you* accept the next call?"

"Hell, they're not after me, they're after you."

"Then why don't I do the telephoning? There's a really attractive blonde over there."

Duffy kicked Sterling gently under the table. "Easy, Pete. We're here on business, remember?"

"Then at least let's have another brew."

Duffy obligingly ordered more *Asbach-uralt*. Sterling downed it quickly and grudgingly accepted the next invitation, but as soon as he had reached the table from which it had come, his heart sank. A fortyish woman of Wagnerian proportions rocketed up from her seat, displayed several gold teeth in a wide welcoming grin and led him to the dance floor, bouncing and giggling.

The next ten minutes were pure torture for Sterling. He followed Duffy's instructions to pretend to speak only English, and since his buxom partner, whose name was Waldtraut, spoke only German, communication was difficult. As though to compensate for this, Waldtraut, grinning coquettishly, grasped him tightly in the manner of a drowning person clutching a lifeguard. They bumped and shoved around the crowded floor, with Sterling shooting nervous glances over Waldtraut's broad, bobbing shoulders at Duffy, who sat snapping his fingers and grinning foolishly.

Angrily, Sterling was now convinced that Duffy had been pulling his leg; it was simply not possible for him to believe that a secret agent was making ready to contact Duffy, especially since Duffy was behaving with such slack-jawed, conspicuous boorishness that at least twenty people, including the headwaiter, were staring at his every movement.

At the conclusion of a set of violent polkas and sambas never seen in Rio, Sterling disentangled himself from Waldtraut and returned to the sanctuary of the table, perspiring and winded.

"You didn't order another drink?" he said.

"Now wait a minute," Duffy whispered. "I know that

46

you're supposed to act like a D.A.F. civilian, but that doesn't mean you really have to get fried."

"Order another round. Or I will."

"Don't you think you've had enough?"

Before Sterling could reply, a bell rang next to his head and a cartridge arrived via pneumatic tube. He took a message from it and read: *Amis who drink too much and insult German girls will get into serious trouble in Berlin. Trüdchen. Table 71.*

Sterling suddenly felt a sobering chill. "It's her," he whispered to Duffy, nodding to a cubicle ten yards to their right. "The girl I met on the street corner the other night. And she's staring right at us, probably has been for quite a while. That booth was empty when we came in. I may be crazy, but I don't like this at all."

Duffy glanced at table 71 and saw a sixteen-year-old girl, her prettiness disfigured by layers of pancake make-up, rouge, and mascara, smirking at Sterling. On either side of her sat two attentive American PFC's; one of them was Negro, the other had Oriental features.

Duffy looked away, plainly not sharing Sterling's concern. "So what?" he whispered impatiently. "This should put your mind to rest, once and for all. If I've ever seen a run-of-the-mill *Ami-Hure*, it's her."

Sterling downed his cognac, and relaxed as its warmth spread through him; it was, he thought, pretty obvious now —how naïve can you be? He crumpled up the note and dropped it to the floor. "Why don't we Amis go home?" he said.

"Not yet," Duffy said. "I haven't made the contact yet." He began to whistle loudly and tunelessly through his teeth as the band struck up a march. The bell rang; another message arrived via pneumatic tube. This time it was for Duffy, who read it, stuck it in his pocket without comment, dispatched a reply, and resumed his off-key whistling.

Sterling began to lose faith in S.I.N, in Duffy's competence and sanity, and in the wisdom of his decision to help out with operational work. The *Resi* had ceased to amuse him; he wanted to leave almost as much as he wanted another drink. They had been here for an hour already, and he had seen no one approach their table, or show the slightest inclination to do so. And the girl was still smirking at him.

The telephone lit up, but when Sterling flatly refused to dance with Waldtraut again, Duffy showed no displeasure. "No action here," he said loudly. "Let's blow." He bellowed for the check, paid it, and left a large tip.

As they drove away from the *Resi*, Sterling said, "Now if I've ever seen a waste of time, that was it."

"Was it?" Duffy said. He took the message from his pocket and handed it to Sterling, who read: *I am here tonight with my Uncle Max. I will return to the Resi on Thursday night alone. I would like very much to see you then. You please me. Hilde Schmalfuss. Table 87.*

"And?" Sterling said, wondering if the cognac they had consumed had gotten to Duffy's brain.

"That's it. What I was waiting for. Uncle Max is our code name for Winter. The message means that Uncle Max —Winter—will definitely arrive at the *Resi*— East Berlin— on Thursday. You please me means that he's all set to defect. Now we'll have to drive up to another club in the French sector." Duffy indulged himself in a self-satisfied smile and there was a hint of irony in his voice as he added, "If this has bored you, you'll get to see a real live secret agent up there. I'm sorry you didn't here, but remember that the M.V.D. didn't either."

They arrived in the district of Wedding, parked near the Gesundbrunnen U-Bahn station, got out, and walked into a narrow, dead-end street flanked by the grey massive blocks of masonry that form the *Mietskasernen*—the rent barracks —of the poorer Berlin working classes.

Duffy led Sterling into the dark central courtyard of a bomb-shattered apartment building and down seven steps from street level to its cellar. He fished a key from his pocket and opened a windowless green door bearing a sign : Belvedere—Private—Off Limits to Members of the Allied Forces.

The Belvedere proved to be nothing more than a long, low, dimly lit room. Its whitewashed walls were bare except for a few photographs of boxers, swimmers, wrestlers, and *Fussball* players, and one large poster of World War II vintage showing a giant ear, underneath which was printed : *"Achtung! Feind Hört Mit!* Attention ! The Enemy is Listening !"

Such light as there was flickered fitfully from candles held in Chianti bottles on the wicker tables enclosing a tiny, sawdust-covered dance floor. Two brunettes, two blondes, and one stunning redhead, all resplendent in 1900 costumes with sequins, ostrich plumes, long white gloves, high button shoes, and velvet skirts slit to reveal a glimpse of black net stockings and scarlet garters, lounged on high stools before a mahogany bar.

The bartender, a sinister looking fellow with a shaved bullet head and tattoos on his muscled, hairy arms, nodded an amiable greeting to Duffy, as though he were an old friend, as he led Sterling surefootedly to one of the curtained private booths lining the far wall.

Six feet from the booth, a Negro midget was playing *Surabaya Jonny* on a white spinet. As Duffy ordered drinks, the stunning redhaired girl slid down from her bar stool, straddled a chair next to the midget and began to sing in a throaty voice :

Ich war jung, Gott, erst sechzehn Jahre...
Du kamest von Burma herauf....

"That's Suzy, the star of the place," Duffy confided. "Sounds just like Marlene, only she's better looking. Good, isn't she?"

Sterling nodded vaguely. He was having trouble focusing on his surroundings, because of the thick smoke, the odour of sawdust, stale beer and cheap perfume, and the jarring effect of the Belvedere's cognac—a fiery potion labelled *Koniak* : Still, he found the girl's casual and melancholy lament more to his taste than the frantic jollity of the *Resi*, and her alabaster skin and fine aristocratic features undeniably attractive. He suddenly thought that it had been six months since he had been to bed with a woman. The thought came out of nowhere, but he did not try to ignore it. This continued celibacy was a pointless gesture, he told himself; it didn't do his late wife any good, and probably contributed to his feeling of boredom and restlessness. He was a man who liked women, always had, and it was futile to try to deny this fact of his life.

Du hast kein Herz, Jonny, und ich
liebe dich so....

The girl sang, stroking and undulating her fine scarlet-gartered legs as she cast sensual glances at a few faces in the hushed audience. Now which of these is a secret agent? Sterling was wondering, when he became aware, with a curious dryness in his throat, that most of Suzy's provocative glances were being directed at him.

Duffy nudged him in the ribs and whispered, "Listen, if she asks you to dance, do me a favour and say yes."

"It will be my pleasure," Sterling said, and got up without hesitation when Suzy finished her turn, sidled over to him, and said in a husky voice that was more of a command than a question, "Shall we dance, *Süsser?*"

Three musicians circled the grinning Negro midget as the wailing rhythms of the *Matrosen Tango* were heard in the Belvedere. Sterling had no difficulty dancing with Suzy; like his late wife, she was only a few inches shorter than he was and able to follow his rusty movements easily; best of all, she made no effort at small talk. He smiled at her tentatively, enjoying the sensation of having a woman in his arms again, and, as his eyes became accustomed to the cave-like murk, he saw the other *Bar Damen* dancing round them with favoured patrons. Then he saw that Duffy had joined the fun.

But he was dancing with a man. He had taken off his green jacket and bow tie and, wearing a pink shirt and an insipid smirk, glided through the sawdust locked in the hairy-armed, ardent embrace of the tattooed bartender.

The odd pair, however, attracted the startled attention of no one except Sterling, who quickly noted that—aside from the *Bar Damen*—all the dancers and the seated customers watching them with bizarre intensity from the shadows were men. Two elderly gentlemen with starched collars and Kaiser Wilhelm whiskers danced past, followed by an American sailor and a Senegalese French soldier, and then Duffy and the bullet-headed bartender again. In his astonishment, Sterling lost rhythm, stepped on Suzy's right instep and stumbled against her large breasts. He was rebuffed by a steel-tipped brassiere and the guttural exclamation, *"Ach, Scheiss!"*

She quickly recovered her poise and embraced him closely in a cheek-to-cheek fox trot. With rising alarm, Sterling now felt her arms and found them hard and muscled under the long white gloves, and, as he brushed her cheek, he felt

51

the unmistakable scrape of beard beneath her powder. When the music stopped, he excused himself and hurried back to the booth.

"What the hell is going on here?" he demanded.

"Not so loud," Duffy cautioned, blowing a kiss to the departing bartender. "Sit down and relax."

"What kind of a joint is this, anyway?"

"Isn't that pretty obvious?"

"And Suzy?"

"He used to be a tank commander in the S.S. Germania Division."

"She's a man?"

"All the *Bar Damen* are transvestites. The blonde near the cash register was a lieutenant-colonel in the British Army until he took his discharge in Berlin last month." Duffy paused. "I wish you'd stop looking at me like that. I've got a wife and three kids."

"Listen, Duffy. I don't like to be played for a sap. You should have told me what kind of a place this was before we came in."

"Cool off. The important thing is that I got what we came for." Duffy lowered his voice until it was barely audible. "Try to understand that we couldn't operate without using homosexuals. They form a world within a world, and they have contacts that are fantastic. That bartender is the cut-out who's in contact with Uncle Max's friend. While we were dancing, he confirmed what I learned in the *Resi*. Uncle Max is coming to East Berlin Thursday, and is definitely going to visit us. Not only that, but he's a much bigger fish than we even suspected. He knows plenty, plenty."

Sterling could not share Duffy's elation at this news, because as he glanced around him, a wave of nausea churned in his stomach. He saw the midget heading toward a back room accompanied by an elderly silver-haired gentleman in

52

pince-nez glasses; a gigantic man with a monocle and dueling scars fondling a simpering youth who could not have been more than fifteen; Suzy, lounging against the bar, regarding him steadily with bright-eyed interest. He had come to Berlin hoping for a drastic change in the scenery available on Orange Grove Avenue, but this wasn't what he had in mind; he had never liked freak shows. "Let's get out of this," he said.

"Why not?" Duffy said. "Our business for the night is finished." He paid the check and they drove back to Dahlem in silence; Duffy, who seemed able to transform his personality at will, was once more the intense, close-mouthed secret agent. He pulled up before the villa on Hindenburgstrasse, let Sterling out, and said, "Be in the office at ten tomorrow, Pete. I'll introduce you to our third and last contact. At the rate we're going, you'll be having your little talk with Uncle Max next week and be on your way back to Arcadia a few weeks after that."

"That will be great."

"What?"

"Nothing. Nothing. See you tomorrow morning."

Sterling left the car and entered the villa. It was dark and empty. He flicked on a light and glanced at his wristwatch; one-thirty. He really couldn't have expected Christiane to be around at this hour. He went to the portable bar and poured himself a generous consolation prize of Jack Daniel's. Then he walked, somewhat unsteadily, up to his bedroom.

What an evening, he thought, as he eased his six feet into bed. He shouldn't complain, though; he had asked for it. But he had not expected espionage to be anything like what he had experienced tonight. Just what he had expected he did not know, but he did know that what he and Duffy had done tonight did not jibe with his preconceived notions of espionage work. Notions derived entirely from the adventure-escape novels he occasionally read for relaxation.

Although he was tired and more than a little drunk, he was again unable to sleep. He was plagued by a vague uneasiness, a realization of feeling a stagnant disatisfaction without knowing why. He found his thoughts, spurred by silence and solitude, drifting toward Christiane. She was no doubt, at this very moment, sleeping soundly above him without a care in the world, or at least secure in the understanding that it wouldn't do any good to worry about such cares as she might have.

He was suddenly gripped by a strong compulsion to get out of bed and walk up to the attic. He wondered what would happen if he did. He raised himself up on his elbows, but sank back again. You won't do it, he thought, just like you won't do anything you really want to do, because you have more common sense than guts these days. Christ, he thought wearily, you weren't always that way; not when you played football for Stanford, not when you married your wife over her parents' strong objections, not when you were flying B-17's in the first years.

He stared at the ceiling, listening to the sound of his own breathing, the only sound he could hear in the dead silence of the Berlin night. Somewhere out there, he thought, out beyond the quite suburbs, Winter is also probably trying to sleep and the secret agents who would soon try to bring off his defection and those other secret agents who, if they knew about it, would surely try to prevent it.

Berlin was quiet, all right, but it struck him as having the ominous, deceptive quiet of an unexploded aerial bomb, buried deep in the earth, still charged and ready to explode if disturbed or handled in the wrong way. A brilliant red dawn flooded his room before he finally fell into a fitful sleep.

5

NEXT MORNING, Ray Duffy kissed his wife at the door of their nine-room house on Faradayweg, drove his three sons to school and went on to the Commissary, where he was employed as a buyer of dairy products for the European Exchange System. It was a good cover; one that permitted him to be absent for long periods of time; one that provided him with a plausible excuse for not keeping regular office hours.

He went through the motions of working for an hour in much better spirits than was usual when he had to go through this boring, but necessary performance. The Winter case was shaping up nicely. The only hint of trouble that he had detected thus far came from an unexpected source: Pete Sterling.

Much as he needed help, he now regretted his decision to involve him in field work. Sterling might be a howling success as an aircraft engineer, but he just did not seem cut out for espionage work; although, Duffy asked himself, how many were? For one thing, Sterling had hit the bottle last night just a little too eagerly for comfort. For another thing, he seemed to have something eating him.

Strange, Duffy thought, for on the surface he appeared to have everything going for him. He was a nice-looking guy, healthy, with a war record that had brought him a few more medals than the usual Distinguished Flying Cross, and that aircraft company he worked for, Duffy happened to know, thought enough of him to pay him eighteen-five a year, Hoping that Sterling wouldn't do some little thing to queer what shaped up as a really good score, Duffy decided to keep a discreet eye on him in future.

He signed his name to an order for Danish butter and left the Commissary. His thoughts shifted from Sterling when he saw two men loitering around his Borgward at the rear of the unguarded parking lot. This was not unusual, but it angered him. Even in broad daylight, these petty thieves who hung around American installations would rifle car interiors, steal tyres, hub caps, jerry cans; they had even been known to make off with Volkswagen motors.

One of them, a dwarfish type with red hair and enormous shoulders, was doing something to the hood of the Borgward right now. Furious, Duffy charged forward, sending them dashing away into Grunewald Forest, the dwarfish man scuttling like a crab after his companion, a tall fellow with pale-blond, wavy hair. Duffy did not give pursuit; he had no time for sneak thieves.

Vaguely remembering something Sterling had said, some figment of his vivid imagination, Duffy checked the Borgward carefully. Finding that no damage had been done, he drove off to the Berlin Base and hurried to his office in expectant excitement. He was expecting a message from K., the East German agent whose cut-out had sent him the message in the *Resi*. Duffy had never met K., who took elaborate precautions and worked through cut-outs, but he had been assured by Irving Hodesblatt, who had recruited him six years before, that K. was a first-rate agent and as trustworthy as any of his kind can be.

According to Hodesblatt, who delved deeply into the backgrounds of the people he intended to develop as agents, and whose resourcefulness never failed to impress Duffy, K. was a Bavarian now in his early fifties. He was the son of circus performers and had himself attained fame as a magician in the 'thirties with a speciality act billed as "K. the Bullet Catcher."

From a distance of eighteen feet, K.'s female assistant would fire a bullet from a ·22 calibre rifle point blank at his face; K. would catch the bullet between his teeth. It was one of the oldest, noblest, and most infrequently mastered of all speciality acts, and had cost the lives of scores of deceptionists.

An early member of the Nazi Party, K. was rewarded during the war with a minor post in the *Ostministerium,* dealing with the occupation of the Ukraine. Hard work, cool nerves, imagination, and a talent for handling people had brought him a transfer to Special Office VI-C-Z of the Reich Security Main Office, where he distinguished himself directing disgruntled Soviet prisoners of war who carried out sabotage behind Red Army lines.

After the war, Hodesblatt somehow came across him, down on his luck, barred from gainful employment by both the Soviet Military Administration and the West Germans, grubbing out a precarious living as a black-market drug peddler. He had eagerly accepted S.I.N.'s offer to return to the sort of work he knew best, and with his experience and contacts, had developed into the leader of a valuable network.

It was a good feeling, Duffy thought, to know that people like K. and Emil the bartender were on your side. If anyone could bring Doctor Eitelfritz Winter out, it was one of those old pros. He flipped a Benzedrine Sulfate Spansule into his mouth and was thumbing intently through the back pages of the *Berliner Tagespiegel* when Sterling appeared.

"Ray," he said. "If you've got a minute, there are some things I'd like to know about Hodesblatt—"

"Not now, not now." Duffy waved him impatiently to a chair and said, "Just got the word from K. One of his top contacts, a major in the S.S.D. detachment that's charged with the surveillance of Winter while he's in East Berlin, has agreed to bring him out personally." He circled an advertisement in the *Tagespiegel* and handed it to Sterling, who read:

LEBENSPARTNER

Contact with eventual partner for life is searched for by a charming young professional woman, 26 years old, 1,66 meters tall, slim, dark, green eyes, of gay and natural character, cultured, speaking French, English, and Spanish. I am looking for "him." "He" must be serious, with wide cultural interests, but also sports and travel-loving, up to thirty-five years of age, with a responsible position, automobile and apartment. Can offer substantial dowry (uncle owns a laundry in Bonn). Send recent photograph and details to Box 1776.

Sterling returned the newspaper with a baffled look. He was also a little annoyed about being brushed off in his attempt to learn something about Hodesblatt, although Hodesblatt didn't really interest him, just his relationship with Christiane.

"K. uses those Marriage Proposals to communicate with us," Duffy went on in a brisk, business-like tone. "It's all right there in code. The major is the Lebenspartner, Winter is the uncle, K. is Box 1776, and so on."

"Now how did you people ever persuade an S.S.D. major to agree to something like this?" Sterling said. His king-sized hangover caused his hand to tremble slightly as he lit a cigarette, and added a note of irritability to his voice. "I mean, what's in it for him?"

Duffy noted the tremor of his hand and thought, this boy does bear watching, he must have had a few more shots after I left him. "The major was a war hero," he explained patiently, "but he was shot up pretty bad. They gave him a lot of morphine and he turned into an addict. We supply him with morphine through K., and over the years he's shown his gratitude in various ways. We've got him hooked, in more ways than one." Duffy chuckled and glanced at his watch. "We're supposed to meet Winter's sister in half an hour and we'd better press on with it," he said. "These people feel insecure if they're kept waiting. We have to assume that her own house is under surveillance, maybe even bugged, so we're meeting her in one of our safe houses over in Schöneberg."

Duffy explained that Frau von Luttwitz, Winter's sister, was no ordinary contact, as they drove to the district of Schöneberg, then crept through an alley and up the back stairs of a decaying apartment building near the *Rathaus*.

"She's a Baroness, real not phony, the widow of a general staff officer," he said. "She lives with an adopted daughter in one of the biggest houses in Dahlem, which, incidentally, belongs to Winter. We repaired the house and kept them both alive right after the war, but now the Baroness won't take our food or money or anything except free gas for her Mercedes. Her attitude seems to be that we're rather uncouth fellows whom she's obliged to deal with to help her dear brother."

Duffy studied Sterling's somewhat flushed face for a few seconds, than said, "Come to think of it, I don't know if it's such a good idea for you to meet her this morning. It might make her suspicious. She's not a pro and we have no real control over her. She's been valuable as a sort of character reference. She writes letters for us to her brother, and she lets us read his letters to her. Since she's his only

59

living blood relative, we can't risk having her do more tha
that or the other side would get suspicious. Here, come i
here a minute."

He led Sterling into a windowless bedroom. "Here's wha
we'll do. This door has a trick window. You can see out bu
they can't see in. Stand here and just watch how I handl
her. I want you to be able to recognize her in case the nee
arises later, and it probably will."

The doorbell rang; three short rings, followed by on
long ring. "That's her," Duffy said, closing the door. Feel
ing a little bit like a Peeping Tom, Sterling peered throug
the window and saw a tall, spare, hatchet-faced woman i
her seventies entering the shabby apartment with great dig
nity, tapping her way forward with a pearl-handled cane
Duffy gave a short bow and welcomed her warmly in fluen
German that had a trace of a Polish accent. His real nam
can't be Duffy, Sterling thought, listening, but then nothin
was as it seemed to be in this business.

The Baroness was followed, unexpectedly, by anothe
woman who was quite a different cup of tea. She was abou
his own age and height, Sterling judged, and she had
platinum-blond hair, heavily rouged cheeks and a chest c
truly Himalayan proportions; her tight, gauzy, sea-gree
dress was cut so low in front as almost to expose her nipples
Duffy nodded to her with cold politeness, but Sterling coul
see anger tightening the muscles of his neck.

The three of them sat down and conversed in low tone
for five minutes, with the Baroness doing most of the talkin
in an excited mumble, and Duffy nodding his head at he
deferentially, Then he suddenly rose and escorted them t
the door. He paused for three or four minutes and then cam
bursting into the bedroom.

"Goddamn!" he said, pounding his right fist into his lef
palm. "That was the Goddamndest dumbest thing I've eve

een. Some of these contacts have rocks in their heads. I've
old the Baroness a hundred times never to bring anyone
vith her. And certainly not that other broad."

"Who was she?" Sterling said.

"That's the adopted daughter. A real weird-ball. I've kept
er out of this case entirely because Winter can't stand her
uts and the C.I.C. report on her would curl your hair.
apparently, she's diddled half the Wacs in Berlin. But the
aroness claimed she wasn't feeling well, wanted the
aughter to drive her to her doctor's, and thought there
vould be no harm in bringing her here on the way. Let's
et out of here. I'll have to have this safe house defrosted
ight away and set up another meeting with the Baroness
omorrow. The old girl must be getting senile. It was a damn
ood thing you stayed in the bedroom."

They drove back to Berlin Base and went to Duffy's
ffice. "Patience," he said. "In this business, patience is
our most valuable asset. To top it off, the Baroness is all
xcited because she read in some paper that if Winter
hould come to West Germany, he'll be arrested as a war
riminal."

Sterling's eyes narrowed. "War criminal. I thought he
vas forced into the Nazi Party?"

"You believe that crap Harry told you about his being
ast a nominal party member? Listen, a week ago one of
ur best subagents turned up some new material on Winter,
he kindly old scientist. Sure he was the one who designed
hose planes for Junkers, just like we had it figured, but in
is spare time he was a consultant to the Institute of
Hygiene of the Waffen S.S. and he was also active with
xperimental Department V at Leipzig."

"What does all that jargon mean?"

"Experimental Department V was composed of chemists
ho tested burn protectants and artificial glands on living

people they got from the concentration camps. Amon
other things, Winter helped design and install those cyanic
gas chambers they used at Auschwitz. Irving Hodesbla
happens to have been born in Vienna, and he's Jewish. F
lost some relatives in Auschwitz, including his father. Whe
he learned about this, he cracked and wanted out of th
case."

"You mean he had a nervous breakdown, that's why I
went back to Washington?"

"All right, now you know. And why shouldn't he hav
cracked? The poor guy was working twelve, fourteen hou
a day on this, seven days a week, for four years. Lister
they may have told you back in Washington that this so
of work is glamorous and a barrel of fun, but there are
lot of aspects to this case that would try the patience of
saint."

Sterling stared thoughtfully through the barred windo
of Duffy's office at the tall, cool pines of Grunewald; the
looked very clean and simple and reminded him of Chris
mas cards, the lost innocence of childhood. "What a way t
make a living," he said.

"Exactly what does that mean?" Duffy said.

"Just that I'm not so sure that I don't agree with Hodes
blatt. Queers, drug-addicts, bald-faced lying, sneakin
around in the shadows and the rest I can swallow. But I'r
not sold on having anything to do with a character wh
designed gas chambers no matter how valuable he is."

The room was filled with an ear-splitting report, as Duff
slammed the file drawer shut and wheeled on Sterling
"Don't pull that moralistic crap on me," he said, with con
trolled rage. "Don't try to tell me you're just finding ou
that espionage is a dirty racket. What did you join S.I.N
for, anyway? I'd really like to know. You didn't think th
was a Girl Scout troop or a health resort or the State de

62

artment, did you? Come off it, man, and be realistic. How
many women and children were killed by those bombs your
-17 dropped during the war? Did you ever give that a
cond thought? Admit that to survive you have to fight,
nd to fight is dirty. Or maybe you don't like to fight any
ore?"

Sterling felt a hot flush at his cheeks. It was the first
me, he thought, that anyone had called him on it, put the
uestion to him baldly, at point-blank range. Eight years
go, another Peter Sterling would have lugged Duffy for
hat remark. But now he just sat there in a confusion of self-
oubt, telling himself that eight years ago nobody would
ave had reason to make such a remark.

Perceptive enough to see that what he had said had
haken Sterling in some strange way, Duffy continued in a
almer tone, "Listen, Pete, admit to yourself that nobody
ares now what this Winter did ten years ago. The only thing
hat anybody cares about is that he's the only one who can
ll us about those Soviet—"

He broke off as he caught sight of a figure in the door-
ay. Standing there with feet wide apart, hands in his
ockets, a pencil behind his ear, was Harry Chute.

"Very nice," he said, with a wry smile. "Very encourag-
g. I'm glad to see that you two fellows are working so
armoniously as a team."

"Sorry, Harry," Duffy said, "but Pete here's just been
aving an attack of ethics. Something about maybe not
anting to interrogate Winter, after all."

"Maybe that decision has already been made for him,"
hute said. "When's the last time you contacted the bar-
nder at the Belvedere, Ray?"

"I talked to Emil only last night."

"What did he have to say?"

"That Uncle Max is arriving tomorrow in East Berlin.

That his group is all set to bring him out, if we want it that way."

"Did he seem nervous, apprehensive?"

"Not at all. He was flying, having a ball."

Chute took out his pipe and lit it. "I had a call from Section IV of the West Berlin Criminal Police while you were out," he said. "Our man over there told me that a corpse was found under the Königstrasse Bridge in Wannsee at nine o'clock this morning. He'd been dead about four hours. Just in case, our man sent me the fingerprints. I checked them against the agent file and they matched Emil's."

"Are you sure, Harry?" There was disbelief in Duffy's voice.

"Well, I couldn't very well go down to the morgue to look at the body without linking him up with us, but there's no doubt that the prints are Emil's. Our man also managed to slip me some photographs."

Chute opened a manila envelope and took from it two glossy eight-by-tens. One of them was a bird's-eye view of a man lying on his back on jagged rocks below a steel bridge; the other was a full-length shot of the same man in the same position. He was dressed in a double vented-suit of white linen; a white silk sports shirt open at the throat and black espadrilles; but for his battered face one might have thought a photographer had surprised him sleeping in the sun.

"He's really a mess," Duffy said. "Do they know how it happened?"

Chute shrugged. "There are no marks on him, other than those that would normally have been caused by a long fall. No bullet or knife wounds, no evidence of strangulation, no trace of alcohol or poison or narcotics in the blood stream, kidneys or brain."

"Probably committed suicide," Duffy ventured. "That's

64

what you get working with homos. They're so damned unstable."

"It's not suicide, Ray," Chute said flatly. "Notice the dotted line marking the distance of the body from the vertical line of the bridge. About twenty feet. Now you may or may not know that a man can't jump horizontally through the air any further than he can jump horizontally on the ground. Taking into account the fact that the wind velocity at the time was sixteen miles an hour, not enough to affect a fall, and that Emil was almost fifty and certainly no athlete, he couldn't possibly have jumped twenty feet. If you can broadjump twenty-six feet, you should enter the Olympic Games."

"I *was* in the Olympic Games, Harry."

Chute grimaced, ignoring Duffy's attempt to treat lightly what he obviously considered a very serious matter. "The way I see it," he went on, "is that somebody beat Emil to death, carried his body under the bridge, and arranged it on the rocks to make it look like he jumped. Or else some chaps held him by the arms and legs and swung him out over the bridge while he was still alive. Some chaps who knew exactly what they were doing."

Sterling stared at the battered face in the prints, the face of a man he had seen alive only last night, and felt his stomach turn slightly; the old serpent of fear snaked down his back. He was a stranger to this kind of violence; you did not see the casualties from a bomber. "Do you think this has any connection with Winter?" he asked Chute.

"It couldn't have," Duffy broke in quickly. "The bridge is in the American sector. Even if the M.V.D. or S.S.D. had burned Emil, they wouldn't have killed him over here. That's the same as sending us a telegram, telling us they know we're after Winter. No, no, this is strictly for the German Criminal Police. Emil was mixed up with blackmailing queers, some of them important people. One of them probably got tired of it. Or else this was a routine mugging. Emil always carried plenty of loot. I'll bet the *Kripo* didn't find any money on him, Harry."

"They found nine hundred marks in his wallet."

"That still doesn't mean anything," Duffy said, but with Sterling thought, less assurance.

"Just that one of your best agents has been sent to Switzerland without any shoes, Ray," Chute observed dryly.

"But not because of Winter. You know yourself, Harry, that the M.V.D. has never killed an American agent in West Berlin, even in the old days. And we still have two other groups going for us. Neither of them has any connection with Emil's group."

Sterling listened to the two professional espionage experts with the deferential silence of the novice, but as he listened a danger signal flashed along the nerve fibres leading to his brain like the dot-dash message of Morse code. He might be a novice, he thought, but something told him that the experts were missing a very important point here.

"K. is a good man," he heard Chute say, "but the Baroness is not going to be much real help."

"K's S.S.D. major can handle the operation alone without any trouble," Duffy said.

"All the same, Ray, I am seriously considering sending a cable to Washington, recommending that we let the Winter case die right now."

"Hell no, Harry. We're too close to back off now. Have you thought about what the other spook organizations will say if we quit over something as vague as this?"

Chute examined the bowl of his pipe with worried thoughtfulness for a few seconds, then looked at the pensive Sterling. "He's unfortunately right on the last count, Pete

Our NATO Allies are very anxious to study the results of your interrogation. The British would never have agreed to call off M.I.5 otherwise. They've always claimed to have better leads than we have. And the Gehlen Organization and the *Verfassungsschutz* will raise hell in Bonn if we bow out, because Winter is a German and they wanted first crack at him. Not to mention Air Force Intelligence, who wanted this for their baby from the start. Have you got any objective comment to make on this, or are you as confused as Ray and I am?"

"Winter is still very much worth talking to," Sterling said. "Even worth taking a lot of risks for, from what I could learn about him in Washington." He paused for a few seconds, trying to find the proper diplomatic words to express the thought that had recently struck his brain with such disturbing impact. "You might consider this, though, about that new information you turned up on Winter's side activities with the S.S. I've just been thinking that he's an aircraft engineer, like myself. It seems odd to me that he would have had anything to do with experiments on people, or designing gas chambers."

Chute had been relighting his pipe; now he stopped, holding a flaming wooden match motionless in front of his chest. Then he raised the match slowly to the bowl of the pipe. "That information was pretty convincing," he said thoughtfully, "but I'll have it re-checked, for what it may be worth. One thing I am certain about, however. I don't want you helping Ray with any more operational work. If there is any queer business going on here, we can't risk losing a man who's helped design some of our new jet aircraft to the other side."

"We're going on with it then, Harry?" Duffy asked.

"With deep reservations and only because we don't have much choice. We'll play it cool, wait for K.'s S.S.D. major to make his move. And remember what I said, Ray. Sterling is out of operational work, as of now." Chute slipped the glossy prints into the manila envelope and left the office.

"Well, that ends your brief career as an espionage agent," Duffy said.

"I wish I could say I was sorry."

"It's just as well. Not because this case has been blown. Harry is way off base on that. But frankly, you're not the type that's cut out for espionage work. That's not a knock. Very few people are, especially Americans."

"Is that bad?"

"All right. I'm sorry I popped off at you before. Forget it happened How about coming over to my place tonight? I'd like you to meet Dolores and my three kids. The oldest one wants to become a pilot."

"I'd like to, Ray, but let's make it another night. Actually, I have something to do tonight."

That wasn't exactly true, Sterling thought, glancing at his wristwatch; the thing he wanted to do, he had decided to do right now. He hurried out of the Berlin Base with a sense of release, got into his B.M.W., and with spirits rising, drove quickly to Hindenburgstrasse.

6

HE DID not find Christiane in the house, but heard the sound of a mower whirring across grass and walked quickly out to the patio. He saw an ancient gardener fighting a losing battle with flat spreading crabgrass, oblivious to the sight of Christiane sunbathing near the rock pool. She was wearing a sort of home-made Bikini and lying on her back on a large towel that was a square of white surrounded by green peacefulness.

He nodded to the gardener, strode over to Christiane and nudged her ankle with his foot. She sat up with an expression that was a mixture of annoyance and puzzlement. "Oh, it's you," she said. "But you told me that you would definitely not be here for lunch today."

"I changed my mind," he said. "Or rather it was changed for me. I've just been fired."

With that remark, he saw, he had at last succeeded in shaking her composure. "Fired!" she said. "You mean you're leaving Berlin?"

"Well, not really *fristlos entlassen*," he said, smiling. "Just relieved of some of my duties. I'll be in Berlin for another few weeks, maybe a month."

Her composure returned, and again he was intrigued by the thought that there must be a number of locked doors lying behind her reserved manner. "What would you like me to make you for lunch?" she said.

"I don't think I want you to make me anything."

"Pardon?"

"I have nothing against your cooking, it's just that I don'
want to eat here. Now that I have some time on my hands
I'd like to see a little of Berlin. It might be my last chance
How would you like to be my guide?"

"There really isn't very much to see in Berlin, any more,'
she said.

"Perhaps not for a Berliner. Look, I know that your dutie
don't include being a guide. But I do have a car, and it'
a nice day."

"Do you really think you'd enjoy driving around an
looking at a lot of ruins?"

Damn, he thought, she's making this difficult. He couldn'
decide whether she really didn't want to go with him, o
whether she was just being coy; he had never been ver
clever about reading women's minds. "There must be some
thing worth doing in Berlin," he persisted. "Make a fev
suggestions."

"Well, they're having the International Film Festival o
the Kurfürstendamm. . . ."

"I don't want to sit in a dark theatre all afternoon."

"But the films are excellent, and you might see som
stars. . . ."

"I wish I cared more, but no."

"You could visit the Zoo."

"Better, but no."

"There's a good art museum here in Dahlem."

"Worse."

"Would you like to take a tour of East Berlin? There's
tourist bus that goes over there every afternoon."

"That's the last thing I want to do."

"I just thought I'd mention it. Americans seem to like t
go there. Why, I don't know. East Berlin is even duller tha
here."

"Then let's forget about East Berlin."

"You could have lunch at the Funkturm and then go for a steamboat ride down the Havel."

Sterling sensed that this was the last suggestion the girl was going to offer. "A splendid idea," he said. "That's what I'll do. Only you'll have to go with me because I don't know where the Funkturm or the Havel is."

They had lunch high up in the restaurant of the Funkturm, which Sterling found pleasant although Christiane made no effort at conversation.

"Have you ever been to Paris?" he asked.

"To Paris? I've never been further away from Berlin than Brandenburg."

"This place reminds me of the Eiffel Tower. A smaller, newer edition."

"The view must be quite different from the Eiffel Tower. That's East Berlin over there."

From his window table, Sterling saw a grey, jagged skyline across the flat plain upon which Berlin was built; for the first time, he realized how close Winter really was. Right now, he was probably having lunch in his hotel, the Johannishof on Friedrichstrasse. In fifteen minutes, he could stroll through the Brandenburg Gate and into the British Sector—if he were only permitted to take such a stroll.

But he didn't feel like thinking about Winter now. Right after coffee, he drove quickly to the landing at Pichelswerder, only to be discouraged by a long line waiting to board the steamer.

"This isn't for me," he said. "Couldn't we rent our own boat?"

"What kind of boat?"

"A sailboat, a canoe, a kayak, anything."

"Do you know how to sail?" she asked doubtfully.

"I think I remember. I used to race a Lightning, years ago."

"If you really know how to use one, you can rent a sailboat over there."

He rented, for an absurdly low price, a twenty-foot Marconi-rigged sloop and sailed the frail craft down a river flowing peacefully between leafy green banks, offering a view of a tower here, a long plane of white café tables there. Before him he could see a curving shore fringed with glittering sands and the wide sweep of a lake upon whose blue surface tiny sails danced like whitecaps. The clean bracing air, the satisfaction of discovering that he still knew how to handle a boat, invigorated him. This, he thought, was just what he had been looking for; it was a long way from the empty house on Orange Grove Avenue, a long way from the Secret Intelligence Network and Doctor Eitelfritz Winter and photographs of a broken body lying on rocks beneath a steel bridge. He began to sing a song called *"eine Seefahrt, die ist lustig."*

"You speak German very well," Christiane said.

"My mother's mother came from Zürich. She helped raise me. And then I kept it up in college."

"I suppose it is helpful in your work."

"Yes, it is," he said, and then wondered if there had been a deeper meaning behind her seemingly harmless statement. But then she could hardly know what his "work" in Berlin consisted of. . . .

"Please, could we stop?" she said. "I'd like to get some sun and go for a swim."

He nodded, turned directly into the wind, slacked away on the mainsheet, then furled the sails, heaved out the anchor and made its line fast to the bow cleat. When he had done this, he turned to see a sight that sent a surge of desire through him. Christiane was poised on tip-toe near the tiller, wearing the Bikini she had worn in the garden. She plunged overboard and swam with strong, graceful strokes away from the sloop toward the strip of soft, white sand that lined the shore.

He watched her, admiring the natural vitality, the pure joy with which she pursued such a simple thing as swimming, regretting that he had not thought to bring a bathing suit. He took off his polo shirt and lay on his back in the cockpit, looking up at the spruce mast swinging in the light across the blue glass of the sky. The sloop rocked on the water that was now still without a ripple, except for the silent passage of an occasional catamaran or canoe.

He felt strangely content and freed from reality and he knew that he could thank Christiane for this feeling of coming alive again. If the girl had made the slightest attempt to interest him, he knew, he would have lost interest in her, or responded with a crude, meaningless attempt at seduction. But she had made no attempt; she made no demands on him, posed no problems for him. She was just there, and that was enough. She was beginning to fill the void in his life, and she was filling it because she was so completely different from his late wife, from everything that recalled the past. She represented that new beginning, the search for which he knew was his real reason for coming to Europe, and the most wonderful thing about it was that she did not seem to realize it.

When the late afternoon sun had begun to turn to gold dusk on the water, Christiane, lithe and brown as a coffee bean, climbed back into the sloop. She stood only an arm's length from him, drying herself, running a towel over the soft contours of her body, down the long curve of her thigh, and he was gripped by a desire for her that was so strong that for a disturbing moment her face swam distorted, as though by intense heat, before his eyes.

"That was fun," she said. His vision became very clear and for the first time, he saw her smile.

"I'm having fun, too," he said. "I'd forgotten how much fun it is to do nothing."

"I wish we could stay out here forever," she said. "Away from people, work, everything."

The remark touched him; it was exactly what he had been thinking. For completely different reasons, he thought, she must feel as alone as I do.

"Could we go sailing now?" she said. "You're very good at it."

"Why don't we just stay here and loaf? There are some things I'd like to talk to you about."

"But it's getting late. And I've never sailed before."

"All right," he said. "We can talk later."

"People talk too much," she said. "Would you turn around, please? I'm going to change this wet bathing suit."

He turned around, pulled in the anchor and unfurled the sails. There is time, he thought. There's no point in hurrying this. He was glad that he had resisted his impulse of a few moments before to take her in his arms; that was not the way to go about it. There was really so much time. He sailed down the narrow Havel River and as it broadened out into the Wannsee, a strong fresh breeze whipped over the stern of the sloop and he let her run past Peacock Island.

Glistening from sun and sea, her lean white hull sliced through the silvery water under a luminous cloud of sail. Sterling, enjoying the quiet graceful drive of the boat, the feeling of being in perfect control of the fickle forces of wind and water, felt wonderfully buoyant and alive. He leaned forward, alert for a slight tremor of the sails, a faint shift of wind, thinking that this was the way life was meant to be. Then he was pleasantly startled to feel Christiane's cool, smooth hand on his shoulder.

He turned around, quickly, expectantly, but saw at once that he had misinterpreted her action; her green eyes were wide and staring straight past his head. "Stop!" she cried. "Stop! Don't you see it?"

He peered through a curtain of spray and saw a motorboat idling low and blackly sinister a few hundred yards dead ahead.

"That's the East German Wasserschutzpolizei!" she cried, fingers digging now into his flesh. "You're heading straight toward Potsdam!"

Cursing, he braced on the cockpit's toe rails and hard against the slanting deck. "Duck, Christiane!" he shouted. "Get your head down!"

As he came about sharply to a starboard tack, the vicious swing of the boom barely missed striking her in the head. She nearly pitched into the water, but he caught her around the waist and threw her back into the sloop. He glanced over his shoulder, relieved to find the patrol boat rapidly vanishing from sight, and was about to see if Christiane had been injured when he was suddenly confronted with another problem.

He noticed with alarm the wind dying, the appearance overhead of low white clouds with dark bottoms, an edge of low thunder beyond the horizon, and hurried to sail the sloop back to her landing, making it just as a violent spring storm swept over the lake and curtained it from view. He and Christiane dashed to the car through mud and driving rain. Soaked and shivering, they drove toward Hindenburgstrasse.

"Are you all right?" he said.

"Yes. But didn't you know that the part of the lake bordering on Potsdam belongs to East Germany?"

"No, I didn't know that."

"What an awful city. One can't feel free here, ever."

"I don't know. You can have a pretty good time in Berlin. At least I did this afternoon."

"You can say that because you don't have to live here."

He was surprised by the bitterness in her voice, depressed by the harsh cutting truth it had just expressed. It was gone now, he thought, the golden moment full of promise, the mood of lazy peace where everything had seemed right, vanished as quickly as the sun, and he was angry with himself for not making more of it while it was there.

"Christiane," he said. "I really didn't know that the East Germans have patrol boats on that lake—"

"It isn't just that," she broke in. "Everything goes wrong here, always. Everything is upside down, people are never what they seem." She stared out at the white gloom of fog and added in a calmer tone, "This city is only good for spies."

He couldn't have been more astonished if the wind had suddenly torn off the car's roof. But he managed to produce a smile and to say, in what he hoped was a casual, bantering tone, "Now what do you know about spies?"

"I'm not stupid, you know."

"I never thought you were."

"Everyone knows that Berlin is full of spies. Irving Hodesblatt was a spy."

"What?" This time, Sterling was unable to keep the shocked alarm from his voice.

"And you want to make love to me, don't you?"

His head spun. The directness of the question, coming with such swift seeming irrelevance on top of the remark about Hodesblatt, shook him. He wasn't prepared for such

76

brutal honesty. He decided to reply in kind. "Of course I do."

"But you never say so. You ask me to be a guide and then take me for a sail and lie in the sun and never say what you really want."

"Maybe that is what I really want."

"Oh, I know you thought it was pleasant out there. There was no hurry. You thought it would be easy later, because, after all, you thought I was sleeping with Hodesblatt."

"Christiane, I don't care a damn what you were doing with Hodesblatt—"

"Well, I was sleeping with him."

He felt a sharp twinge in his chest which made him realize that he did care. Where had it gone, the radiant hour? he wondered. But his present mood of deflation was his own fault. He had made the old mistake of trying to make this girl conform to his image of the perfect woman, and she had turned out to be just a woman and not a convenient player in a romance of illusions. But this only made him want her more, and he was intrigued by this sudden compulsive need of hers to talk, to lash out at him. Why should she do this, he thought, if she didn't have some feeling toward him? He couldn't believe that their close call with the patrol boat, frightening as it was, was the only reason for the sudden disintegration of her usual cool reserve.

"Did Hodesblatt tell you he was a spy?" he said, trying to treat the incident as a joke. "I didn't know him, but I heard that he had some sort of routine job with the Quartermaster Corps. Overseeing blankets, furniture, things like that."

"You do think I'm stupid," she said. "Don't you realize that nobody in Berlin is stupid? We can't afford it. Do you want to know how I know these things?"

77

"No, I don't. I don't happen to want to listen to any hard-luck stories right now. I don't want to hear how the Amis bombed your house and the Russians raped you in a cellar and you sold yourself for a chocolate bar. I believe it and it's too bad but it really doesn't matter. . . ."

"The Russians never bothered me," she said. "I was twelve when the war ended and I was living on a farm in Neu Ruppin. None of those other things happened to me, either. I was lucky. I even was accepted at the best design school in East Berlin. I did very well. When I was nineteen, my professor called at our apartment. He told my mother and father that he had a very interesting proposition for them. He said that he was really a member of the secret police and the head of an organization that employed girls to sleep with foreign diplomats and then report on what they said. The professor said this work was extremely well paid and would require a few nights' work a week and would be a great service to the state. My father nearly threw him out of the apartment, but my mother said that I should accept the offer. I wish I could hate her, but she's a little crazy. The professor came back the next night and I came to West Berlin. I got a job as a waitress in a place where I had to wear a Bavarian dirndl and carry three beer steins in each hand. That's where I met Hodesblatt. He was so nice. He asked me if I'd like to be his housekeeper. I came to Dahlem with him and slept with him after a few weeks, though he never insisted, and I don't think he enjoyed it very much. He was a strange man, very melancholy. Have you ever slept with anyone just because you feel sorry for them and they're good to you? Then one night he asked me if I would like to carry some messages for him to East Berlin when I visited my parents. So you see, he, too, wasn't what he seemed. Nobody is here. I said I would, but then he began to act very queerly and finally had a nervous breakdown. Why should that happen if he just had some routine job with the Quartermaster Corps?"

Suddenly she fell silent and the familiar mask of composure settled over her face. It disturbed him more than what she had just told him. No one so young, so pretty, he thought, should have eyes that are so old, so resigned.

"I don't know anything about spies," he said, "but I doubt that Hodesblatt was one. I suspect that he had some black market contacts in the East Sector and wanted you to carry messages to them."

She shrugged. "What difference does it make? You don't even know what I'm talking about."

He pulled up before the villa on Hindenburgstrasse and they dodged inside out of the wind-swept street. They had left the windows open and the house was cold. "I'd better start the fire," he said. "Do you want some cognac? It will warm you up."

"I don't drink," she said. "But you do. I've noticed the empty bottles."

"You're not the only one with problems, Christiane."

"What problems can a man like you have?" she said, savagely. "What can you know about problems?"

"You're one of my problems," he said, trying for a lighter tone, disturbed by the sudden atmosphere of tenseness. I don't want it to be this way, he thought; I like this girl too much, I don't want this day to disintegrate. "Look," he said. "I really don't feel like a drink, either, thanks to you. I want you to know that I had a wonderful time this afternoon. And I'd like you to go upstairs now and dry off and change and then have dinner with me. We'll go to some nice place with an orchestra and try to laugh a little. . . ."

"Is that what you'd really like to do?" Her green eyes fixed him with a look of challenge and, he thought, a jarring hint of contempt.

"No," he said, quickly. "No, it isn't."

"Then why don't you say what you want to do! Why do you have to be like everybody else!" Her voice, loud and shrill and edged with a strange exciting mixture of contempt and pleading and fury, was cut off as he moved to her quickly, took her in his arms, and kissed her hard on the lips. Her lips were firm and cold, but the warmth of her struggling breasts shot through him like a current. He kissed her again and again, her lips now moist, warm and slowly opening, and he thought that she was so right, that it was senseless to evade doing what one wanted so desperately to do, and then he wasn't thinking anymore, just feeling, bursting out of his old tired shell of anxiety and boredom and futility into a bright timeless world where nothing mattered but to be alive.

7

STERLING AWOKE near dawn conscious of a chilly wetness against his face. A fine spring rain was being blown though the open window next to his head. Reluctantly, he got up and closed the window, then turned back to the bed, saw that Christiane was still sleeping, and slipped in gently beside her. It was a humid night, and now that the window was shut, the scent of her perfume was very strong. He rested on his side and regarded the girl as she shook off the constricting linen, watched her deep and regular breathing, watched the rise and fall of her breasts held in the liquid embrace of the faint dying rays of the moon.

He had never, he thought, seen a woman so simply beautiful. He bent over the snowbank of flesh and very lightly kissed her shoulder, brushed the mass of dark hair from her forehead. Suddenly he felt like waking her, and was unreasonably impatient when she failed to respond.

Then he saw the hint of a smile form on her lips. Had she, he wondered, been awake all this time? He became certain of it when he recalled having closed the window last night. She must have awakened before him and opened it again to the chilling rain. The implications of this excited him.

Then still smiling, but without opening her eyes, or speaking, she drew him to her, finger tips digging into the hollow of his back. He had no time to think, only to act, to enjoy, before it happened again, better this time but again much too quickly and he fell back pleasantly exhausted. But even as sleep claimed him, he felt like a man awakening.

When Sterling awoke again, sunrays were slanting across his face and the place beside him in the bed was cold and empty. The momentary shock, the sharp sense of loss he experienced because of Christiane's absence decided him. He jumped up, threw on his bathrobe, and hurried downstairs. He found her brewing coffee in the kitchen, came up behind her, threw his arms around her waist and kissed her neck.

"How would you like to live in California?" he said. "Married to me?"

Her quick reply jolted him from his euphoric trance. Instead of being surprised or elated, she said, matter of factly, "Don't you live in Washington?"

"No, near Los Angeles."

"But don't you work for the government?"

"Only temporarily."

"You have a civilian job in California?"

"Yes, I have a job." He smiled. "I train seas lions at Marineland. But what's that got to do with it? Answer my question."

"You were serious?"

"Quite serious."

"I don't believe it. Don't joke about a thing like that. It's cruel." She turned away from him, but before she did so, he thought he noticed a tear on her cheek. She has every reason to be mistrustful, he thought, remembering what she had told him about her life yesterday. He tried to take her in his arms again, but she shook him off.

"You don't have to say that because of last night," she said, with a violence that startled him. "I'll stay with you here until you leave. That's what you want isn't it?"

"No, Goddamnit, that isn't what I want! If you think you're the only attractive girl I can get to sleep with me, you're dead wrong." With an effort, he paused, lowered his voice, and continued in what he hoped was a more reasonably persuasive tone, "Listen, Christiane, this is not a joke or a crazy whim. I'm not a screwball or a kid. I know exactly what I'm doing. I love you and I want you to marry me. I need you, probably a lot more than you need me. There's absolutely no reason why we can't be married. If you still think I'm joking, we'll start getting whatever papers are necessary first thing Monday morning."

"When would we be married?" Although there was less doubt in her voice, it was still there.

"The day after my job here is finished."

"When will that be?"

"A month, maybe less. Frankly, I'm ready to give it up right now, but I have an obligation to stay that long."

"A month is a long time."

"I won't change my mind."

"Is your job here so important, if your real work is in California? What do you do here, anyway? Tell me, please."

"I'm doing a routine survey for the Air Force. I'm an aeronautical engineer." Christ, he thought, what a business espionage was; it even required you to lie to the woman you wanted to marry. "My job isn't so terribly important," he went on. "There's a good chance that I can wind it up a lot quicker than in a month. I'll know for certain early this week."

"I would have to tell my family."

He had forgotten that formality, perhaps because he had no family of his own. "Of course," he said. "Where do they live?"

"In Prenzlauer Berg." She paused and looked at him thoughtfully. "I have a good idea. Why don't you come over with me and meet them?"

He experienced an unpleasant twinge of suspicion; this

was the second time she had suggested his going into the East Sector. He quickly dismissed it, thinking that espionage really was a delightful business when it got you into the habit of suspecting everyone's motives as a matter of course. "No," he said.

"But why not?"

"I just don't happen to want to go into the East Sector."

"I don't understand why. There's no law against your going there. Hundreds of Americans go there every week."

"Christiane, let's not have our first argument over this. I'd love to meet your mother and father and I know it's the normal thing to do, but I won't go into the East Sector. Why can't you invite them over here. . . ?" He checked himself, thinking that even this was a bad idea.

"They wouldn't come," she said, to his great relief. "My father is a party member and works on the Stalin Allee project and they might report him."

"He's a party member?"

"Oh, he isn't really a Communist. At least, he hasn't been since 1945. But he had to join the party to keep his job."

Now where have I heard that before? Sterling thought. "Why doesn't your father just pack up and come to West Germany?" he said.

"Because he's afraid. He's become like everybody else, afraid to say what they mean, do what they want. He owns a small apartment that wasn't hit in the air raids and he does have a good job as a master mason and he's lived in Prenzlauer Berg all his life. He's a real Berliner. He says that at his age he doesn't want to go to West Germany like a beggar and sit around a refugee camp with a lot of strangers. He's given up. Now he's just a *kleiner Mann* who doesn't want any more trouble. Oh, I don't really mean that. I do love him, but I don't expect him to be more than he is."

84

"Well, I'm sorry about not being able to meet him," Sterling said. "Maybe it will be possible some day. Do you think he'll object to your marrying me?"

She laughed. "Object? How can he object? He knows that there is nothing for a young girl over there. I don't care about my mother, but I must tell him."

"Then I think you should do it as quickly as possible. You'll have to apply for papers at the consulate and that may take a long time. I mean, since you do come from the East." She's too young to have had any connection with the Nazis, he thought, then said, "You never had to become a member of any Communist youth organizations, did you?"

"No," she said, again with a vehemence that gave him a mild start. "I hate politics. I hate clubs and organizations that make one wear uniforms and flat shoes and march and behave just like everybody else."

"So do I." He smiled. "Well, that makes it easier. But you really should let your mother and father know right away."

"I could go today. They'll be home."

"No," he said. "I don't want you to go today. Tomorrow will be time enough. I want you with me today. I'm tired of being alone on Sundays."

8

But sterling did not let Christiane go to East Berlin on Monday because he had heard on the radio that there had been a minor flare-up of violence on Block C-South of the Stalin Allee project during Friday's lunch hour. The workers there had protested against a 10 per cent raise in their quotas; there had been some scuffling with party officials; some of the workers had walked off the job; there was even talk of more violence to come.

Christiane did not think much of this possibility. "You don't really think the government would permit a real strike?" she said. "They probably organized the whole thing just to prove that the workers have some freedom now that Stalin's dead."

Sterling had to agree with her. He simply couldn't bring himself to believe that the workers of East Berlin had the courage to stage a genuine strike against their government. The odds against them were too overwhelming, and he had a cynical, melancholy lack of faith in people doing anything against great odds. When Monday passed without major incident, and most of the workers had trooped back to the Stalin Allee with their usual docility, Sterling agreed that Christiane should leave first thing Tuesday morning.

An hour after dawn, he drove her to the French Sector and walked upstairs with her to the platform of the Gesund brunnen S-Bahn station.

"I don't see why I have to leave this early," she said, as

hey waited for the train that would take her to Prenzlauer
Berg.

"Because I want to get this over with as quickly as possible. Do you have all your papers?"

"You've asked me that twice already."

He lit a Chesterfield nervously and said, "I'll see you
tonight about seven, then? Right here on the platform?"

She smiled at him and said, "Peter, why don't you just
get on the train with me? It's only two stops. We could be
there in fifteen minutes."

He shook his head.

"But I really would like you to meet my father," she
insisted.

"I'd like to meet him, Christiane, but I can't go with you
now and that's all there is to it. As a matter of fact, I'm beginning to wish that you wouldn't go, either."

"But I must, this one last time."

"I understand that, but there must be some other way to
let your parents know. I just don't like the idea of your going
over there."

"You mustn't believe everything you hear about East
Berlin," she said. "There's no danger for unimportant
people like me. I've made this trip hundreds of times."

Before he could say anything, the train came along. She
kissed him, pushed her way in, and then vanished in a
wedge of grey shapes, but as the train pulled away he caught
one glimpse of her, smiling at him, her face vibrant with
life in a sea of dull, flat, anonymous faces.

Now that she was gone, his old feeling of emptiness returned. He went downstairs and drove to Kurfürstendamm,
where he tried to kill time window-shopping. As he peered
through the plate glass window of Horn's he was rather
startled to see the Baroness von Luttwitz's adopted daughter
trying on a hat; he had never thought that she would be an

early riser. Though he knew that there was no need for it, he hurried away to have coffee on the terrace of the Kranzler.

The city around him, where so many things had happened but where nothing seemed to happen anymore, seemed particularly quiet to him this fine morning. The sidewalk cafés were mostly empty, traffic was desultory, and the Film Festival flags hung limply from their poles; he could only hope that East Berlin, where Christiane must be by now, was this somnolent.

Across the street, above a motion picture theatre, a huge, garish poster stared down at him : *Heute—Lohn der Angst —La Salaire de la Peur—The Wages of Fear*. Perhaps, he thought, I'll come back to see that tonight; a few hours of vicarious violence might help the time pass more quickly. He saw the Baroness' adopted daughter emerge from Horn's, hatless, her platinum blonde hair glinting in the sun, paid his check and left.

When he had regained the house on Hindenburgstrasse, he could not bear the prospect of sitting around alone, doing nothing but counting the hours until Christiane should return, so he called the Berlin Base and asked for Mr. Cabot; this was one of Ray Duffy's many cover names.

"Do you think I'll be needed today?" Sterling asked.

"No. We don't expect much business at the PX."

"Then I think I'll go boating on Wannsee."

"Good idea. Fun in the sun."

"You're sure it will be all right?"

"Positive. The shipment of Danish milk won't be in for a couple of days. But I still say it will definitely get here."

"I'll call in again around four."

"Don't bother. Business is really slow. Have yourself some fun while you can, you only live once." There was an impatient edge to Duffy's voice. "Anything else?"

"No."

"All right. Just don't get hung up on any sandbars. I still want you to meet my Uncle Max." Duffy hung up.

Harry Chute did not arrive in his office until ten-thirty that morning; this was remarked on because he made a fetish of punctuality. The first thing that he did was to buzz for Ray Duffy. The first thing he said was, "Ray, forget about Uncle Max."

"What?"

"The case is closed." Before Duffy could protest, Chute went on quickly, "I followed up on that idea Sterling had and found that those documents implicating Winter in war crimes had been forged and planted where one of our agents would be sure to find them. I also discovered that someone planted a newspaper story about Winter's being arrested if he came to West Germany."

"Is that all, Harry?"

"No, that isn't all. A gardener found K. this morning in the Tiergarten. He'd been shot throught the mouth with a Beretta Plinker ·22." Chute permitted himself a tired smile. "'K. the Bullet Catcher.' Whoever killed him not only knew him, but had a sense of humour. I wish I knew who his last audience was."

Duffy stared at him in stunned disbelief, and Chute continued in a relentless monotone, "They found the body of the S.S.D. major near his, face down in the water at the edge of a small pond. He hadn't died from drowning, but from an overdose of morphine. I think we used to supply him with enough for about 0.1 grams daily to keep him happy and working for us. This time he took, or someone forced him to take, a fatal dose. The *Kripo* says about 0.16 grams.'"

"Then it's obvious what happened," Duffy said. "The major tried to pressure a bigger supply out of K. and when he refused, the major shot him, then conked out himself. It's a hell of a note, but why should it mean we have to drop Uncle Max?"

"Come off it, Ray," Chute said, with some exasperation. "There can no longer be any doubt about what has happened. You know it, and I know it. The Winter case has been blown. I don't know how ... yet ... but it's been blown sky-high."

"I can't buy that, Harry. The pattern doesn't figure at all."

"Of course it doesn't figure. Nothing that has happened has any logic to it at all. If they wanted to stop Winter from defecting, all they had to do was to keep him under light surveillance in Dresden. Why let him come up here? Why all these murders, and why in West Berlin where we'd find out about them right away? The M.V.D. doesn't murder people for the hell of it; they only use the *Istrebiteli* as a last resort. But whether their actions make any sense or not, they've penetrated this operation and we're dropping it as of now. And as if I didn't have enough to worry about with this, there are some odd things going on over on the Stalin Allee project."

"I heard about that. It doesn't mean a thing."

"I'm not so sure. It could mean trouble for our communications with the zone."

"What trouble? The People's Police will let them blow off steam, then crack a few heads, and that will be that."

"I hope you're right. In any case, you won't be around to see if your estimate of the situation is correct."

"What does that mean, Harry?"

"I want you to find Sterling and I want both of you to take the four o'clock military flight to Frankfurt this afternoon. I won't even risk sending you by commercial carrier. I want you both back in Washington by tomorrow night."

90

"Harry, I'm meeting the Baroness for lunch!"

"The Baroness will be buying her own lunches in future. Ray, don't fight me on this. I've seen eight years of hard work sucked down the drain this morning. And because this one case has been blown, we'll have to change our cover, remount all our other operations, screen all our agents. Perhaps you haven't fully understood what I'm trying to communicate. There is not the slightest chance that we can get Winter now for interrogation. That's a damned shame, but I can live with it. But from the crazy pattern of this case up to now, I'm convinced that they are going to try to kill two more of our people. That would be you, and Sterling. Now find him and get on that four o'clock flight."

Duffy seethed with anger as he drove down Potsdamer Allee toward Wannsee. He felt no fear at the possibility that persons unknown to him had marked him down for murder, first of all because he did not believe that this was true, and secondly because he was confident that he could protect himself. When he had been an O.S.S. officer during the war, leading a band of Polish guerrillas behind Wehrmacht lines on the Oder River, he had done some killing himself, with nothing more than a pencil or a rolled newspaper. Let them try, he thought, just let them try.

He was far more concerned about his future than the vague dangers of the present. He was furious at this abrupt end to his hopes for quick career advancement. He had seen in the Winter case a long-awaited opportunity to break out of the minor league of Polish Covert Operations into German Covert. Now he pictured himself crouched behind a desk in Washington, glassy-eyed from reading piles of dull reports fighting the battle of the water cooler and five o'clock traffic, and he grew steadily more angry.

What had gone wrong? he wondered. It had all seemed

so beautifully set up. Had Winter been pulling S.I.N.'s leg all along? Had Emil or K. been double agents? Had one of the desk men back in Washington taken one too many martinis and talked out of turn? Had Sterling. . . ?

Here an ugly suspicion arose in Duffy's mind. What about Christiane? She knew Hodesblatt and she knew Sterling and she knew him. The C.I.C. check rated her clean, but that was no guarantee.

No longer quite so angry or confused, Duffy pressed down on the accelerator. The Borgward responded to 60, 70, 80 kilometres an hour. If he could locate Sterling quickly and question him about Christiane, and then get hold of Christiane herself, it was not impossible that he could find some answers that would make it unnecessary for him to leave Berlin operational work. At 90, 100 kilometres, the car raced easily down the wide, tree-lined avenue, barren of traffic because it led to nothing but the Potsdam checkpoint.

It was only when Duffy had reached 110 kilometres an hour that the steering wheel began to quiver. With his sure instinct for trouble, he slacked off on the accelerator. 100, 90, 80. The wheel wobbled and then spun crazily in his tightening grip. He pulled his foot from the pedal and with a rush of fear—fear such as he had not known since his parachute had almost failed to open over the Oder River— he grabbed for the handbrake and pushed down on the footbrake. Neither responded. The car, completely out of control, raced forward like a rolling coffin.

He clawed open the door, but before he could leap out, the Borgward veered right, missed a fire hydrant, and jumped the curb at forty kilometres an hour. Then something cracked and he was snapped like a whip, snapped as in the opening shock of a parachute magnified a thousand times, snapped into a wine-red cement curtain.

He was unconscious when the Military Police scooped him out of the wrecked car forty-five minutes later. He regained consciousness as he was being wheeled into the emergency operating room of the 279th Station Hospital.

He sensed that he wasn't going to die. He knew that he wasn't going to die because he could see clearly, because he could think clearly, too clearly. And what he was thinking, with feelings of impotence and horror, took his mind away from his own numb and broken body, his wife and his three sons.

The surgeon standing over him marvelled at the ability of the human body to survive punishment. And, as he listened to Duffy's clear but disconnected speech, he also marvelled at the odd things that patients would come out with in a state of drugged shock.

"Before you operate," Duffy said, "I've got to contact my office. . . ."

"Later, later," the surgeon said.

"Now. . . . Harry was right . . . they are going to try to kill Sterling. . . . I've got to warn Sterling!"

"Of course you do," the surgeon said patiently. Odd, he thought; then, anxious to get on with the difficult operation, he motioned forward an anesthetist in a green skull-cap.

"Sterling . . . kill him . . . the *Istrebiteli*," Duffy said, and then, as the cone was placed over his face, he died.

PART TWO

The Exterminator

1

BEFORE LEAVING his shabby hotel near the Wildpark Station in Potsdam, the Exterminator informed the manager that he was going on a tour of Sanssouci, followed by dinner with a business prospect, and would therefore not be taking his evening meal at the hotel.

The manager smiled and wished the Exterminator—sincerely—a rewarding afternoon. For the manager considered him a model guest: he paid his bills on time, tipped well, never complained about the slipshod service, and was in general so pleasant and unassuming that the manager had decided he could get away with padding his final bill.

And yet, for all his unobtrusiveness, he puzzled the manager. He had registered with a Hungarian passport, yet he spoke fluent German with the trace of a Silesian accent. He had listed his occupation as "business; export-import," yet he did not seem to pursue it with noticeable zeal. He remained in his small room all day, going out only at night. He made no telephone calls and received none; posted no letters and received none; and had no visitors of either sex. Odd, the manager thought; but then, since the foreign tourists had ceased swarming into Potsdam every summer, he had learned to be grateful for any paying guest and tolerant of bizarre habits.

Waving goodbye to the manager, the Exterminator, carrying a small tan canvas beach bag, strolled off into the nearby park of Sanssouci. In his pockets were a small bottle

97

of chloral hydrate, a larger bottle containing a colourless liquid, and an absorbent cloth; more than enough, he reasoned, for the assignment at hand, which was "render harmless American Agent S-27 (Peter Sterling)." He was not otherwise armed, for he considered firearms the tools of the amateur.

He was not an amateur, any more than his occupation was "business; export-import." His name was Benno, and he was a major attached to the Potsdam *Avanpost* of the Ninth Section for Terror and Diversion of the M.V.D. Only two weeks before, he had been an instructor at the advanced school operated by the Ninth Section in a large country house at Kuchino. Here, promising graduates of the school for apprentice executioners on the corner of Turnaninsky Pereulok and Metrostroyevskaya Street in Moscow were groomed to become agents of the Mobile Groups for Special Tasks, *Istrebiteli*-Exterminators.

Benno was considered one of the more valuable faculty members. Because he had done all these things flawlessly himself, many times, he was particularly adept at teaching students how to break every bone in a man's body without killing him; how to extract confessions quickly by use of the electric needle; how to administer just the right dose of strychnine so that the victim's head would bend back almost to his buttocks in violent tetanic seizures.

Benno was now about forty-five, at the complacent summit of a distinguished civil-service career in which he had exterminated seventeen enemies of state in places ranging from Shirgaz to Yucatan. He was a few inches over five feet and pear-shaped. His narrow shoulders and chest widened out to flabby hips that undulated slightly as he walked. A few sparse hairs ornamented the crown of his skull, which was of an odd shape bearing some resemblance to a crooked elbow. His appearance and his soft, purring voice, fluent n six languages, suggested a plump and wary cat.

He strolled on without haste through the bright summer's
ay, pausing to admire a statue here, a floral arrangement
here, a short, round solitary figure wandering past the Fas-
nerie, the Charlottenhof, the Roman Bath, and the Great
'ountain. At the Green Railing, he met two men as if by
ccident; it seemed like the chance encounter of long-lost
riends.

They sauntered out of the park, got into a long, black,
re-war Horch parked near the Weinberg-Tor, drove to a
arage in an empty side-street, changed their clothes and
lrove off again, with Benno at the wheel. He drove quickly
ow, for he knew that Sterling would have to be dealt with
nmediately; to wait for the cover of night would be un-
wise, for by this time his organization must have finally
uessed what was going on and would try to send him
ome. Fortunately, he had been placed under round the
lock surveillance and it was known exactly where he was,
xactly what he was doing.

This intelligence had come through only fifteen minutes
efore on the transistor radio concealed in Benno's alarm
lock, and had closed with the command: *Put into effect
lan B.* Glad that this Special Task was nearing its end at
ist, amused that its success stemmed from a lead supplied
y a most unlikely source—a German girl—Benno increased
ie Horch's speed as it left the suburbs of Potsdam for the
ungfernsee.

His two assistants sat beside him, silent and impassive as
sual. Benno gave them a quick, contemptuous side-long
lance; he regarded them as little better than common
riminals, mercenary thugs. He did not even know their
eal names or their nationalities, which were unimportant
» him in any case. They were simply tools, he thought,
»ecially selected for this one job from some strange store-

house, placed at his disposal like the cigarette case he had used last month in Prague. When opened, it had fired dum-dum bullets coated with potassium cyanide; it had accomplished its purpose, and required no further thought; his two assistants would accomplish their purpose and he would forget them as easily. .

The tall lean one with the pale-blond hair he guessed to be a Rumanian, judging from his accent and his fondness for swilling *Tsuica*. His one outstanding talent was a fluent knowledge of English, gained—it seemed—from nine years spent as a pimp in Soho. As for the red-haired, dwarfish one, it was impossible to know anything; he had a serious speech impediment, the result, apparently of some bad beatings taken as a carnival wrestler in Bulgaria.

Still, in all fairness, Benno had to admit that these two had followed his instructions well and were more than competent at the brute physical violence which he preferred to leave to the less skilled. The dwarfish one had worked over Emil the bartender quite expertly with the length of rubber hose, and the tall one had been surprisingly expert with Mr Duffy's car last night. In a masterly fashion, he had pulled out a cotter pin and loosened the nut on the king-pin which held in place the tie-rod connecting the two front wheels to the steering mechanism. He himself could not have done better.

Benno stopped the car in the weed-grown parking lot of an abandoned lake-side café and walked with his two assistants to a landing. As he waited patiently for them to make the sailboat ready, he spied some herbs with finely-cut leaves small white flowers, and fleshy roots resembling carrots fringing the banks of the lake. No doubt about it, he decided, with the quiet joy of the connoisseur; those innocuous herbs, glowing with health and beauty in the sunshine were water hemlock and contained a toxin both virulent and horrible and more lethal than strychnine. He found the paradox poignant, and curiously intriguing.

The arrival of the sailboat interrupted his reverie. Before boarding it, Benno peered out over the Jungfernsee to where it flowed into the Wannsee. The rays of the morning sun struck violently upon the still flat surface of the water, shattering themselves into a sparkling dust that made his eyes blink and water. He searched his pockets for sunglasses; he had never liked the sun.

Sterling was sailing the eastern shores of Wannsee in a fifteen-foot gaff rigged sloop and being very careful not to repeat his mistake of blundering anywhere near that part of the huge lake controlled by the East Germans. The inner city had reclaimed the weekend's mob of picnickers, bathers, and sailors, and he had the wonderful feeling that he had at his disposal a private sea.

It was sunny, crisp and clear, with a strong breeze. Beaufort Number 6, he estimated, the sort of weather in which the wind could be heard whistling in telegraph wires. He had never felt better in his life, and congratulated himself on having found such a safe, and satisfying, way to kill time until Christiane's return.

Ever since Harry Chute had ended his brief career as a secret agent, he thought, he had been living in what was for him a novel, and pleasant, kind of limbo. For three days, he had not read a newspaper, worked, or thought of anything much except Christiane. Now, somewhat guiltily, his thoughts drifted to Doctor Winter. The subject, so important to him a week before, now seemed as remote as the sleek thirty-five-foot sloop which he saw a thousand yards to his starboard.

Still, he found himself hoping that S.I.N. would discover that it had made some mistake about Winter's being a war

criminal and go on to manage his defection. A solid interrogation of Winter, together with his discovery of Christiane, would add up to a gratifyingly successful Berlin assignment, and there was no doubt in his mind that the old man
remained an intelligence source of tremendous potential.

But, he thought gratefully, the skulduggery necessary to
get Winter out of East Berlin was no longer his concern. He
glanced at his wristwatch, calculated that Christiane would
be back in only seven hours and twenty minutes, and then
had his attention diverted by the odd handling of the thirty-
five-foot sloop, which had now approached within three
hundred yards to his starboard.

It was difficult to ignore her, for she was the only other
craft on the water, except for a few canoes barely visible on
the horizon. He judged that her crew must be heading her
too close to the wind's eye, for her sails were luffing and she
was not moving forward. Sterling observed this inept performance with a twinge of annoyance; it always disturbed
him to see a fine boat abused by novices.

With mounting alarm, he saw her suddenly head off; her
mainsheet was slacked off, the boom swung out violently,
and then the jib sheet tore loose from the clew of the sail and
the mast quivered as though it were about to snap. He saw
a red sweater being waved on an oar, heard a foghorn blow,
and, thinking only of giving assistance, he came about and
sailed alongside the sloop. He was about to drop his own
sails, when he caught sight of the three men in the boat
opposite his.

One of them was resting, with great unconcern, against
the pole of an American flag attached to the bow. He wore
only shorts and white rubber shoes, and the sun shone on
his pink knobby knees, glanced off his sunglasses, gleamed
dully, like a caution signal, against the yellow belt buckle
which dug deeply into the greyish swell of his stomach.

Then, with a sudden chilling shock of recognition, Sterling saw, grinning at him and calling for help, a short man with curly red hair, long ape-like arms and enormous shoulders, and another man with pale-blond, wavy hair, his lean frame dressed in the uniform of an American sailor. Quickly, without knowing exactly why, but knowing as he had never known anything before that he had to get out of there, away from those two weird shapes he had encountered on his first night in Berlin, Sterling moved his tiller and bore away on a starboard reach, heading, not for the far off landing float, but for the nearest point on shore.

He held course without looking back, telling himself with immense relief that whatever they were after, they had no chance to overtake him without a jib sheet and with damaged rigging, until he heard a faint but familiar sound that caused him to snap his head around.

He saw that the sloop had dropped so far behind that she looked like a plastic toy, but that he had not succeeded in completely losing her, though her sails were furled. He heard the noise again, realized with a sudden rush of panic what it meant, and saw the sloop start to knife through the water, looming larger and larger as she bore down on his stern.

Unarmed, defenceless, knowing that he was unable to outrun his strange pursuers, he was gripped by the strangling fear of a small boy who sees himself in a dream, trapped in quicksand as some nameless slimy terror slithers toward him, the choking fear of a twenty-five mission pilot caught in a sky of red flak just once too often. Within minutes, his frail craft was rocking crazily in the wash of the sloop's concealed 100-h.p. inboard motor as she sped by, circled him twice, and slowed down to come alongside.

A cockney voice commanded him to anchor, but he refused to obey; the shore was only minutes away and he was determined to try for it. He heard a brief hammering like the noise of a pneumatic drill, looked and saw the dwarfish man pointing a machine pistol at him. A different fear surged through him. They were not out to kill him. If they wanted to cut him down, nothing could be easier, out here on the shores of a peaceful lake where only the sun and azure sky were witnesses. But they had deliberately avoided killing him; they were after something else.

He ducked down with his hand still on the tiller until another burst from the machine pistol shattered the rudder, tore holes in the hull through which water oozed. He was sent sprawling by a collision, heard a rending scrape and the clank of grappling irons, saw the dwarfish man beckoning to him from the other boat with the snout of the machine pistol. Acting on the wild chance that he would not fire, Sterling snatched up an oar and swung it, felt the crunch of bone along the wood, saw crimson spread over the sloping forehead as the man pitched backward, screaming into the water.

Before he could position the oar again, the tall, blond man leaped into the boat behind him; had tightened one arm around his windpipe and dug a thumb into the brain stem at the base of his skull. Through searing pain, he heard a thump and the patter-pat of another pair of feet, felt a cloth pressed against his mouth and nostrils. Struggling wildly, he smelled something sweet, tried to bite the hand through the cloth and tasted something sweet. His arms and legs began to feel leaden; the sun shattered into a hundred dazzling, blazing suns and then re-formed into a single cold black monstrous sun that was the last thing he saw.

2

WHEN STERLING came to and opened his eyes, his brain throbbed as though it were being struck repeated blows from the padded mallets in a piano action. He shut his eyes and the throbbing persisted, though with less intensity.

Making a great effort of the will, he forced his eyes open and endured the renewed pounding. He saw that he was lying flat on his back on a cot consisting of three wooden planks, still dressed in white linen slacks, pink polo shirt, and blue Italian rope sandals. Only his wallet and wedding ring were missing.

Supporting himself on his elbows he made out a cell ten by fifteen feet. Its bare walls were clean and smelled of formaldehyde. A thin film of brackish water covered the stone floor and he judged that he must be below ground level. That was all he could be reasonably sure of, for there were no windows; he did not know whether it was night or day or how long he had been here.

The only light glowed dimly from a forty-watt bulb in the ceiling. There was an upended metal bucket in one corner. His throat was parched and he craved water, but there were no faucets in the cell. With aching limbs, he struggled to his feet and to the door. It was steel, with a six-inch square opening, painted green. Sterling ran his hands over the steel, but could feel nothing; the nerves in his hands seemed dead.

He peered through the opening into a hazy corridor lined

with cells; these did not have solid steel doors, but iron bars. He could make out grey shapes behind the bars, and hear someone whistling tunelessly, compulsively, over and over again :

Mei' Muatterl War A Wienerin. ...

He sank back on the planks, trying to think clearly, to make some sense out of his predicament, but could not. It had all happened too quickly. And it was absurd. It was fantastic. Things like this happened to other people, but not to people like him. For the past few days, he thought, he had been living in a dream, and this was just an extension of that dream.

His right arm flapped over the side of the cot and to the floor and his hand felt something soft. For a horrible instant, he thought that he had touched a human hand. He bolted to his feet and saw a rat—fat and lazy with age—scuttling off to varnish behind the metal bucket. A terrifying shock of illumination swept his mind clear. He knew now that it had really happened; the dream was dissolving into the beginnings of a very real nightmare. He fell on the door and punded its unyielding steel with his fists.

Almost immediately, bolts were drawn and two guards entered brandishing submachine guns. They backed Sterling to the cot and clamped a circlet of steel connected to the wall by a brass chain around his neck. Then they stepped back and came smartly to attention as a short, pear-shaped man padded into the cell.

Although he wore civilian clothes and did not wear sunglasses, Sterling recognized him instantly. His attention was caught by the man's brown eyes, which moved while the baldish head, topped by a few sparse pink hairs, remained

106

stationary, a detail which made Sterling regard his visitor as not so much frightening as weirdly comic.

"My name is Benno," the man said, in a soft, purring voice. "I am an officer in the Soviet State Security Service. We will speak English because I want to talk to you privately for a few minutes. The guards do not speak English and neither does Warden Sauer of the East German State Security Service who will be here shortly and into whose custody I am instructed to transfer you. We will speak English, even though you speak German very well, don't you, Mr. Sterling?"

"Leck mich am Arsch—" Sterling's words died in blinding pain as Benno gave a vicious pull to the chain attached to the circlet of steel around his neck.

"You are also a spy," Benno said, matter-of-factly, fondling the length of chain.

Choking for breath through the searing pain, Sterling still felt a sense of shock at the accusation. Good God, he thought wildly, I'm not a spy, of all things I'm not a spy.

"Do you deny that you are a spy?" Benno asked. He jerked the chain again, but almost gently this time. "You piece of ordure! Of course you deny it, but we know all about you. We have known all about you since your first night in Berlin."

Benno released the chain, sat down on the metal bucket, and peered into Sterling's face. "Now I am going to tell you what is in store for you," he said. "We are turning you over to the East German officials, since it is their legitimate government you have tried to befoul with your criminal activities. They will interrogate you, just as you hoped to interrogate Doctor Winter. First they will find out all you know about the American jet aircraft. Then they will find out all you know about the activities of the gangster Western espionage organizations. Then they will give you a public trial in which you will confess in the presence of Western correspondents to criminal espionage activities against the German Democratic Republic. Your life will be spared, but you will be sentenced to life imprisonment and hard labour in the uranium mines at Aue. An example will be made of you for the world to see. And you will confess at this trial, because you have no choice. You cannot escape, you cannot be rescued, you are completely alone, and you *are* guilty of espionage!"

Benno got up from the metal bucket and glanced at his wristwatch. "Therefore," he continued, "it would be wiser for you to co-operate with us from the beginning. Especially since the man in charge of this prison is Warden Sauer. He was once a Gestapo interrogator at the well-known Rue Lauriston centre in Paris, but even the Gestapo found his methods of persuasion too extreme. They transferred him to Buchenwald, where he was a *Blockführer*. Do not make the mistake of trying to resist him. . . ."

The steel door opened and a man six-and-one-half-feet tall entered. He had a rotund frame, red nose, ruddy cheeks and snow-white hair, and he reminded Sterling, again in a weirdly comic way, of a department store Santa Claus. He fondled in his right hand a small magneto alternator; from it dangled two long thin steel wires, their terminal points the grasping jaws of tiny steel pincers.

"This is the American spy, Sauer," Benno said, in German.

"So. So," Sauer said, in a jolly voice redolent of cigars and beer. He advanced on Sterling and made as if to fix one of the toothed clips of the wires to his wrist. Sterling twisted away as an ague of sudden fear gripped him, fear such as he had never known, fear so strong that it completely blotted out his pain, fear that made him doubt himself and his ability to deny these men what they wanted.

And one grim corrosive truth kept eating at his brain, adding to his fear; he was a helpless victim, but if they were charging him with espionage, far from an innocent one.

Benno impatiently motioned Sauer and his magneto alternator away. "Not now," he said. "I want to talk to you, Sauer." He turned to Sterling. "Goodbye for now, Mr. Sterling," he said, in English. "While you have these few moments to yourself, think about my advice. It is of no purpose to resist."

Benno padded out of the cell, trailed by Sauer. They walked to the warden's office, where Benno took Sauer's leather chair, leaving him to stand. "Do you have the papers of transference ready?" he asked.

"Yes, sir," Sauer said. "Right here."

"You've certified that he was alive and in good health when I turned him over to you?"

"Yes, sir."

Benno read the documents carefully, signed his name, kept one copy, and said, "Well, he's yours now."

"Yes, sir. He's ours now."

"But that doesn't mean that you can do anything with him that you like. Remember that you must not kill him or disfigure him. He must appear in good health at his trial. The plan is to transfer him to the sanatorium in Leipzig in a few days. The doctors there will find out all he knows and see to it that he co-operates at his trial. Do you understand?"

"Yes, sir."

"I'm going to have something to eat now, and then I'm going over to the Johannishof to see if Doctor Winter is in the proper frame of mind for his speech at the University tomorrow. I'll be back in a few hours to ask the American a few questions about the activities of his organization, things that can't wait for Leipzig."

Benno rose and without saying goodbye to Sauer, waddled out of the office with a sense of relief. Prolonged visits to prisons made him feel restless; he disliked being in any confined space. And he always felt a little uneasy in Sauer's presence. The warden, he thought, considering his record at Buchenwald, was surely an authentic case of a monster in human form, although he was now forbidden to go to the extremes which had been encouraged in the concentration camps. What could it be like, he wondered, to be at the mercy of Sauer, or someone like him. . . .

Although he had just completed a smoothly executed operation, almost a model of its kind, Benno was not in his normally complacent mood; he was, in fact, not happy at all. He knew, from past experience, that he would not be thanked for what he had so faultlessly accomplished. His superior, a beefy colonel with a strident voice and an overbearing manner, would, as usual, take his efficient performance for granted and then claim all the credit at the Directorate. He would not be rewarded with the promotion which he felt was long overdue, nor even with so much as a few days' leave. On the contrary, the colonel would probably give him a dressing down about the death of the dwarfish man, or about some equally petty detail. Nobody appreciated him, Benno thought, nobody.

But the reasons which prevented him from experiencing his usual sense of satisfaction went deeper than this. The rumour that he had heard days before, and which had worried him into sleeplessness, appeared now to have been fact. Fantastic as it might seem, there were reliable reports circulating that Beria, chief of the M.V.D., had been arrested and was even now in the cellars of the Lubianka in Moscow. And he, Benno, had been brought into the service by Beria, and was known as one of his men.

But as soon as he had walked out into the summer sun,

blinked his eyes, and drunk in the fresh air, he felt less anxious, less insecure. He was worrying without reason, he thought. After all, one had to look on the brighter side of things. No one could deny that he had done his usual competent job, and there must be officials at the Directorate who realized his worth, who knew how difficult it would be to replace a man of his proven skill and experience.

He walked along, blinking his eyes in the sun, thinking of Sauer, and then blotted out this disquieting image with speculation about his next assignment. The only certainty which the future held for him was the certainty of a new assignment; for agents of the Ninth Section for Terror and Diversion there would always be fresh assignments.

After Benno had left, Sauer relaxed in his leather swivel chair and looked up the latest football results in *Neues Deutschland. Blue-White,* he read, had defeated *Alemannia,* 3 to 1.

He balled up the newspaper and flung it to the floor. Damn! He had had fifty marks going on *Alemannia.* He had no luck at all, he thought. He could not understand why he had never once in his entire fifty-two years been able to win a football wager. It was irritating. On the miserable pittance which they paid him—even taking into account the graft from commissary supplies—he could ill afford the loss of fifty marks. He poured himself some of his favourite *Weisse mit Schuss* (mild light wheat beer with a shot of raspberry syrup), considered Benno, and his mood grew even darker.

He thought of him with a twinge of fear, for he had heard that the fellow, harmless looking though he was, was not only a "people stealer," but a professional executioner, a murderer on an international scale. One had to be careful around a chap like that, deferential. Still, he had no call to treat him in that contemptuous way. M.V.D. officer or not, he could observe the rules of common politeness; but then he was a Russian, what could one expect?

Growing steadily more angry, Sauer fingered the rubber truncheon which he always kept on his blotter, as other men might keep a letter opener. He drained the large glass bowl of beer, then tossed the remains of a ham sandwich to a scarred, black-and-tan Doberman pinscher at his feet. The Doberman wolfed it down, then submitted with surly resignation to a few affectionate pats on its serpentine head. Sauer gingerly wiped his mouth with the back of his hand, eased his bulk out of the chair, picked up the truncheon and said, "Come, Dirk."

He walked slowly, deliberately (there was no hurry) to the basement, with Dirk padding at his side. The eighty-pound dog came up to his hip; one of its eyes was blood-shot, the other had been lost in a fight. Sauer scorned body-guards; wherever he went in the prison, he went alone with Dirk, hoping that a prisoner would dare to resist him, or even to attack him. None, he thought with contempt, had ever tried; they were all scum, sheep, as fatalistic as Moslems.

He entered the dim, dank basement cell block, whose in-mates recoiled from iron bars and fell silent at his approach. They were all accused of sabotage or espionage; members of the Fighting Group Against Inhumanity, the Gehlen Organization, N.T.S. Sauer could do what he liked with them, and they had learned to know it.

He passed them by, walked to the isolation cell, peered through its peephole and saw the American, eyes closed, lying on his back on the wooden planks; the guards had removed the circlet of steel from his neck.

For a brief anxious moment, Sauer wondered if he had died. There would be the devil to pay if that had happened.

But no, he thought, that was impossible; he was just weak, hungry, thirsty. Suddenly, recalling that one of the after effects of chloroform was to leave a man with an intense craving for water, he had an intriguing idea; he fetched a tin cup, pushed it through an opening at the bottom of the door, and tapped on the door with his truncheon.

Sterling heard the tapping and almost cried out when he saw the water. His throat burned, the roof of his mouth felt like dried leather, swallowing was a minor torture. But he hesitated to snatch up the precious liquid; suppose it were poisoned?

But no, he thought with melancholy relief, that, at least could not be true. They did not want him dead. He stared at the cup, weakening and cursing his weakness, rushed to it and pressed it to his lips. Then, tasting the salt with which the water had been laced, he spat it out. He heard a booming laugh, looked at the peephole, saw a pair of eyes staring at him and flung the cup.

Sauer fell back with an obscene shout of rage and incredulity, rubbing his eyes. A sound new to the cell block welled up in his ears. Laughter! They were daring to laugh, and at him! His blinding fury, however, was tempered by a strong feeling of acrid pleasure as he fumbled open the cell door with a physical joy that could be read in the pallor that spread over his ruddy cheeks, his hands clenching and unclenching, smoothing and stroking the sweaty hard rubber of the truncheon.

The pleasure became almost unbearable as he hesitated, stepped aside, and called out a command. Obediently, its diamond-shaped ears tense, the Doberman pinscher bolted in just ahead of him.

3

STRONG HANDS lifted Sterling, gentle hands cooled his brow with a wet rag. Through a grey mist of pain, he saw the fragments of a figure form and blur. He pressed his eyes shut, fought hard to concentrate, to clear away the sudden doubt that his mind had become unhinged, that he was seeing things, opened his eyes again and saw the fragments come together. Bending over him was an American PFC, tall, gangling, with a shock of mustard-coloured hair, a friendly grin, two rows of coloured ribbons on his chest, the word KOREA on his left shoulder patch.

"You're an American?" Sterling said, wild hope welling up within him.

The soldier stared back in surprise. "Hell, yes. You an American, too? I didn't know they wuz arresting United States civilians now."

Sterling looked beyond the soldier and saw that he was still in the same cell, after all; there was the rat squatting on the metal bucket, eyeing him sleepily.

"Name's Bob Munger," the soldier said. "What's yours?" Very gently, he resumed patting Sterling's forehead with the cool rag.

"Sterling. Peter Sterling. Would you have any water? Water to drink?"

"Sure thing." Solicitously, Munger raised Sterling's head and pressed a tin cup to his lips. The water was cool and unsalted and Sterling had to fight hard not to swallow it all at once.

"What the devil you doing in here?" Munger said.

"I don't know. . . . I don't know."

"Well, I know what I'm doing in here," Munger volunteered cheerfully. "I sneaked into East Berlin to sack in with my *Schatzi*. She's got a place in Johannisthal, right across the sector border. I got a little stoned on her old man's *Steinhäger*, got into a fight with three of them blue Vopos and the bastards tossed me in here. How do you like that? Been here maybe a week. How about you?"

"I don't know," Sterling said. "A day, two days, twelve hours."

"You look like you been here longer than that. Sauer didn't set his dog on you?"

Sterling nodded. The water was gone.

"That's his favourite gag," Munger said, pounding his right fist into his left palm. "I've seen him take that hound's muzzle off and let him tear people apart. Least he didn't go that far with you." Munger paused reflectively. "Someday that guy will get his," he added, without much conviction. "You sure you don't know what you're in here for?"

"No."

"I heard somebody say something about *Spion* in the exercise yard. That means spy in Kraut. Man, I hope they don't have you tabbed for a spy."

"I'm not a spy."

"They're rough on spies. They don't pay much attention to burglars, or rapists, or drunks like me, but they're awful hard on spies. This whole basement is filled with people they think is spies. Figure how crowded it is when they got to stick two people into a cell this size. Damn if I know where they expect both of us to sleep. Guess they don't care. Say, you don't have much to say, buddy."

115

Sterling stifled a wild, irrational impulse to laugh. "There really isn't much to say, is there?"

"Now don't go thinkin' that," Munger counselled. "That's what they want. They want to beat you down, turn you into a zombie, make you figure nothing matters anymore. Don't let 'em do it. Things ain't so bad. Look, you got a friend now. I'm your friend. Ain't I your friend?"

Sterling nodded.

"So that means you ain't alone," Munger grinned, sitting down on the edge of the cot. "As long as you got a friend, somebody you can trust, somebody you tell your troubles to, there's still hope. Right?"

"I suppose so."

"You sure you don't want to tell me what you did to get into this? Might make you feel better to talk about it."

"I have nothing to say." Sterling tried to sit up, but could not manage it.

"Reason I thought you might want to talk about it," Munger persisted, "is if I get out of here before you I could tell your friends on the outside. Then they could help you."

"I haven't got any friends on the outside."

"Buddy, you don't have to con me. I mean why? Listen, I heard about this real top spy outfit in Dahlem. I heard on the prison grapevine that they're organizing a big revolt in East Berlin—"

"Heard on the grapevine?" Sterling broke in. "You understand German?"

"Sure I speak Kraut. My old man came from Essen and I've shacked up off post with my Schatzi for two years. I heard that this revolt is for real. It started on Friday, down on the Stalin Allee project. Listen, if you're tied up with this spy outfit, and they knew you were in here, they could get you out. Man, I heard *they got ways* to do things. If

116

they could stir up a big revolt, hell, they oughta be able to do a little thing like springing you from here."

No, Sterling thought, he can't be a plant. He can't be. He's too obvious, too dumb, or whoever sent him is. And now that he knew something about the realities of espionage work, the suggestion that S.I.N. had the power, the expertise, to rescue him from this prison, much less organize a revolt against the East German government, struck him as so painfully ludicrous that he again had to stifle the impulse to laugh. "Munger," he said. "Please believe me. I'm glad they put you in here with me. I don't know who you are, but I do know that I'm glad to have another human being to talk to. But I have nothing to tell you. I can't think straight now."

"Small wonder, if Sauer was working on you." Munger peered intently at Sterling. "Best thing to do with him is let him have his own way. He ain't hardly human. He don't care what he does. The stories I heard about that guy. Last Christmas he had them put up a really beautiful Christmas tree, right in the centre of the exercise yard. He let the prisoners come out and look at it. But he made them stand looking at it in the snow without any shoes, singing damned Christmas carols until they dropped. He's got a great sense of humour. They put some gypsies in here. Sauer got them to form an orchestra. Every time he gives a prisoner a lashing on the *Bock*, he has them standing by, fiddling away with them gypsy songs. But the worst thing he's got is the 'Bath-tub.' "

"The Bathtub?"

"Sauer's got a special room where he's got this big old bathtub. If he's got it in for a prisoner real bad, he ties him up, puts him in the tub and turns on the water. He's got the thing rigged up so he can make the water boiling hot or freezing cold. I'm telling you these things so you don't wise off at him. He don't like to be crossed. Just do what he says. Say, buddy, you must be hungry. I got some German pineapples, if you want some."

"German pineapples?" Sterling felt particularly stupid, falling into the habit of dumb repetition.

"Turnips. That's what they feed us here. That and horse-meat stew." He handed two turnips to Sterling; they were tough as wood, but he managed to eat and keep them down.

"Thanks," Sterling said.

Munger shrugged his shoulders. "No need for thanks. I'm your friend. Got a Gold Dollar cigarette, too, if you want it."

"I couldn't taste tobacco now. You seem to be in good spirits. Considering everything."

"I got reason to be," Munger said, with a sly grin. Sterling noticed, for the first time, that he was slightly wall-eyed, and a little old for a PFC, about forty-five. "I'm your friend, right?" Munger went on. "We're in this together. You trust me and I trust you?"

"Yes." What else, Sterling thought, could he say?

"Then I'm going to show you just how big a friend I am." Munger paused, then suddenly gripped Sterling's hand and pressed his lips against his ear. "I got a set of keys," he whispered.

"What?"

"Not so loud. I tell you I got a complete set of keys to this joint."

"I don't believe it." The thought flashed upon Sterling that his new cellmate was a lunatic. Then Munger produced a cord to which were attached seven paraffin wax keys. Sterling found himself jerking up to a sitting position. "Where did you get them?"

"From a guard. This place is lousy with graft. I made friends with this guard who wants to go over to West Ger-

118

many. I told him I'd give him some money and put in the good word for him with the Army if he'd help me escape."

"You mean you really think you can get out of here?"

"*We* can get out of here. There's no doubt about it. I've been planning this for five days—even got a little map of the prison. Are you game?"

Wild sweet unreasoning hope possessed Sterling. He tried to stand, fell backward onto the cot, tried again, wavered on his feet for a few seconds, then sank to his knees. Tears of frustration scalded his eyes.

Munger helped him to his feet. "Come on, buddy. Try. You got to try. We make the break now or never. My guard friend has this post. He might not have it again for a week. You got to try, man."

Munger released Sterling, who, though his muscles cried with pain, managed to stay on his feet. After five excruciating minutes, he began to shuffle back and forth, back and forth.

"Great," Munger whispered. "You got guts, buddy. Now take off your shoes. Just follow me and don't make any noise. The other prisoners will see us, but they'll keep quiet. I'd like to let some of them out, but only the two of us got a chance to make it." He turned a key in the lock, swung open the heavy steel door, and put his arm around Sterling. "I told you I was your friend. Trust me, and we'll be out of here in half an hour."

They crept down the yellow, glazed brick corridor, opened another door, and crept up a twisting flight of steps to a third door. Munger opened this and came face to face with the barrel of a submachine gun held by an elderly, wizened guard. The guard lowered the gun, winked at Munger, and they walked on.

For the first time, Sterling began to take heart, to believe in his new friend and his surrealistic escape plan. In this nightmare world where everything seemed possible, he thought, why should this be impossible? Hope acted on him like a shot of adrenalin, clearing his head, loosening his muscles and making them respond. Even if they did not succeed, any straw was worth grasping at to avoid another clubbing from Sauer, and what would come after.

They gained a fourth door. Munger opened it and they found themselves suddenly walking into darkness. Sterling heard a booming laugh; lights blazed, and he saw that he was in an enormous windowless room, its steep walls lined with foam rubber. There was nothing in the room, except for a wooden chair, and next to it a long, white, old-fashioned bathtub. He heard the disembodied laugh again and then saw Sauer, followed by Benno and two guards, step out of the wall.

"He was trying to escape," Munger said, in fluent German.

"*So*," Sauer said. "*So*."

"He admitted he was a spy. But he won't talk."

"We'll see about that. Get out, leave us alone."

With a vacant smile on his face, but without looking at Sterling, Munger withdrew. The guards grabbed Sterling, pinned his arms, and hustled him into the chair.

"Now," Benno said, in a soft voice. "I'm going to ask you a few questions. If you answer them, no harm will come to you. Do not try to be a hero by refusing to answer my questions. There are no heroes in this prison. Who is the chief of your organization in West Berlin?"

Sterling muttered an obscenity.

"Really, we have no time for this," Benno said, with a grimace. He snapped his fingers, the two guards lifted Sterling out of the chair, and Sauer strolled over and rapped him across the testicles with the end of his truncheon. Doubled up with pain, Sterling was stripped by the guards

120

and hustled, struggling wildly, into the bathtub. Benno clamped a bronze grille over the tub and turned on a tap; lukewarm water seeped into the tub, inching up around Sterling's chest, then around his neck. It had the strange effect of easing the throbbing in his groin, of reviving him.

"Who is the chief of your organization in West Berlin?" Benno asked.

The water oozed up around Sterling's lips. He raised himself on his elbows, struggling to push his face up against the grille and the air beyond it. A hideous feeling of hopelessness, of helplessness surged through him; he felt nakedly alone, trapped in a watery coffin, and he had to bite his tongue to keep from answering.

"Answer me, please," Benno said. "We already know who your chief is, but I want to hear you say it."

The water which enveloped him like a liquid shroud now began to turn cold, and made Sterling tremble with fear. His arms aching, he managed to keep his head barely out of the water and gasp for air. His mind began to stray into strange realms. He pictured himself, in a few months' time, as a familiar stock figure; standing—pale, blinking, and apologetic—before an East German judge, droning out a confession. How could he hope to escape playing this final role, he wondered with blank despair; why even attempt the impossible?

He felt his will to resist being eaten away by a stream of thoughts that poured over his mind like a corrosive, unstoppable acid. He thought, with a leaden guilt, of his late wife, of the mess he had made of his life since she had died. His oppressive sense of personal failure was sharpened by the thought that the world he lived in was also pretty much of a failure. He had once believed in progress, the essential goodness and perfectability of man, and above all in reason, and yet centuries of cerebration seemed to have resulted in

121

nothing more than a rising radiation count, Benno, Warden Sauer and his 'Bathtub'.

And what could he think of the poor submissive wretches who were in this prison with him, and the millions of other poor wretches in the larger prison outside these walls? How could he seriously believe that man was not an aimless stranger in a meaningless universe when confronted by their grey fate, and their dumb abject acceptance of it? If only he could believe that there were a few among them who had the guts to stand up and say—NO! But there were none; they remained as hopeless and trapped as he was in this medieval torture chamber from which there was no escape.

The thought, however, that most sapped his will to resist came from a more personal source. He had been betrayed, there could be no doubt of that. Had Christiane done it? Much as he fought against this suspicion, it now seemed plausible that she had been the one. And he had loved that girl, foolishly, stupidly, but he had loved her. And he had been certain that she had loved him. If this love could be so easily counterfeited and betrayed, it was difficult to believe that anything mattered anymore.

"Answer me, please," he heard Benno's voice repeating softly. "Remember that this is only the beginning. Remember that you are alone, completely helpless. Your Government cannot help you and would not if it could, for to admit your existence would be to admit that it is engaging in espionage. And you are not even worthy of your government's assistance. You were sent to Berlin on an important assignment, but since your arrival you have done nothing but engage in a sordid liaison with a German girl. You are weak, Mr. Sterling, and you have been betrayed. You are alone. Answer me, who is the chief of your organization in West Berlin?"

Sterling's will to resist shrivelled with Benno's last words. Benno turned a crank on the side of the bathtub and the grille lowered over Sterling's face, pushing him down under the water. He was plunged into a world as black as his feelings of despair and futility. His eardrums pounded and almost burst and he could only wonder weakly why they still bothered; they didn't have to anymore.

The grille was raised and Sterling brought his head up, more from a reflex action than any strong desire to breathe, to go on living. "Answer me, please," he heard Benno's voice, as though from far away, insisting. "Why undergo this when it is not only unnecessary, but futile? We know where your *Freundin*, Fräulein Christiane Stock, is right at this moment. She is in Prenzlauer Berg and S.S.D. agents have just gone to arrest her, to bring her here. All of you have been caught. Why should you continue to resist? It is pointless. Answer me, please."

Sterling reached up and caught the grille with his fingers, shaking it with a wild impotent rage. Intense hatred and anger burned within him, dissolving his uncaring despair of a moment before, protecting him from fear. Good God, he thought, it hadn't been true. Christiane had not been the one. And now they were going to arrest her, bring her here. His fingers, clutching at the grille as at life itself, slowly loosened.

"Answer me, please," Benno said, with a touch of impatience. No answer came.

"Answer me!" Benno turned a tap; the water turned ice-cold.

"Answer...."

No answer came. After forty minutes, Benno turned away in disgust. "He's fainted," he said, matter-of-factly. "Have him taken out of there before he drowns, Sauer. These primitive methods are really quite unsatisfactory. Put him

123

in solitary and keep him awake. I'll return in the morning. You can use your magneto then. But the doctors and the drugs are the only answer to this problem."

Benno padded to the door. "Strange," he said. "I was sure that he was about to talk at one point. This is not going to be as easy as I thought."

His swollen face streaming with sweat, Sterling lay on his back in a new humid cell so tiny that he could not stand up. A white light, relentless and inescapable, seared his eyelids and drained his brain. How long had he been here? he wondered. His body was no longer racked with pain; nothing felt broken; he was simply numb, and fortified by the discovery that pain, once endured, could not be remembered and experienced again.

But he could not attain that sleep necessary to preserve sanity, to permit him to escape for a while from the waves of slow rollers that were pounding at his brain, isolating him from the shores of reality. A grating record, an old Prussian marching song, boomed through the cell, its rattle of drum rolls and clashing of cymbals played over and over again.

Sleeplessness, he thought, his mind wandering, was as grim a torture as any devised. He began to see a halo around the searing white light, then a million black umbrellas opening and closing on the wall. Thick grey cobwebs clung to his face and hands and he tried frantically and without success to wash them away.

The faint bark of a dog and a shuffling of feet at the far end of the corridor brought him back to reality and he stiffened. The brief pause in the desert was over, he thought wearily, Sauer must be coming again, and he was no hallucination. He experienced a sudden flash of virulent hatred and desire for revenge that he had never thought himself capable of as a rational man. It strengthened his determination to continue to resist, to pit himself against the mindless brutality that Benno and Sauer represented.

It would be a futile, lonely triumph, he knew, but he was sure he could achieve it. They did not want him dead, he thought, that much was clear. Therefore the torture could not be carried to its logical end; they would always have to stop, somewhere. And he was no longer afraid. He had been sick with fear only hours before, but he had survived it and crossed an invisible border into a state of mind where he had left fear behind forever.

He turned on his stomach in a vain attempt to escape the searing white light and waited. More waves of disconnected images surged through his fevered brain. The first trainer he had soloed in, a sailboat racing past a green island, a wrecked car on the Hollywood Freeway, a girl swimming away from him. He thought with infinite sadness and quiet rage of Christiane. Where was she? Were they bringing her to him now, to torture her in his presence? To resist the kind of evil that could do such things seemed to him the most important challenge he would ever face in his life.

Still waiting, he again heard the dog bark, and the curious shuffling noise, growing louder now, in the normally still corridor. He waited, thinking that the only thing he could do was wait, and husband his failing strength.

4

CHRISTIANE REACHED Prenzlauer Berg without difficulty forty minutes after leaving Sterling. Her parents lived in a huge block of stone, in an apartment which they had bought thirty years before. Alone of the buildings on its treeless street, it had escaped aerial bombardment, although its flaking grey walls were pitted by small arms fire. The Stock family was well housed by East German standards, but then Fritz Stock was a master mason who worked regularly and earned good wages plus an occasional bonus.

Christiane felt an almost physical loathing as she neared the apartment where she had been born and where she had grown up. She hated the three small rooms, the musty furniture, the cheap oil paintings of Alpine scenes, the view on the dark central courtyard, the everpresent smell of cooking in the halls. Ever since she could remember, there had been *Vertrauensleute* living in 1-A, reporting on the activities of the other tenants, first under the Nazis and now under the Communists.

She climbed the four flights of stairs and rang a bell. It did not work, so she knocked. After a long wait, the door opened slowly to reveal her mother peering at her in myopic astonishment.

"*So*," Frau Stock said. "You're back." She was a tall thin woman, worn by toil and her share of the vicissitudes experienced by most Berliners of her generation. Looking at her angular, pinched face it was hard to believe that she had produced the accident of beauty that was Christiane.

"Is father home?" Christiane said, stepping inside.

"What do you care where your father is?" Frau Stock said. "All you ever think about is yourself, and having a good time with the Americans."

Christiane sighed with a patience learned long ago and offered a blue canvas bag to her mother. "I brought you some nylon stockings and soap from the American PX. And some cigars for father."

Frau Stock brushed the bag aside and sank into a horsehair chair. "We don't want anything from you. Why didn't you stay with your Americans?"

"I came to see father."

"He's not here now."

"I know that, but he always comes home for lunch."

"He won't be home today."

"But I must see him."

"Then go to the prison!" Frau Stock almost shouted. "It would be a good place for you!"

"Father has been arrested?"

"Haven't you heard about the trouble at Block C-South on Friday? Some of the men protested the raising of the work norms. Father struck an *Aktivist* and the S.S.D. arrested him." Frau Stock began to sob and twist her bony hands in anguish. "The fool! He could never behave reasonably, like other men. Always talking, arguing. A little man trying to act like a big man. . . ."

Frau Stock stopped short when she heard a rapping on the door. She stared at it as though it were about to explode. "They've come for me now," she whispered. "They've come for me. Don't answer it. Pretend we're not home. Pretend we're not home."

Again the rapping, loud and insistent now. Christiane, numb with shock at the news of her father's arrest, could

only stare at the door as dumbly as her mother. Then i
swung open and Fritz Stock walked in, still wearing hi
white mason's overalls, a grin creasing his round face. He
was a short, barrel-chested man with large, strong hands,
jug ears, and iron-grey hair; a yellowish welt had appeared
over his left eye. Frau Stock sat staring at him in frozen disbelief, but Christiane ran up and threw her arms around
him.

After a long family lunch that took on something of the
nature of a celebration, Frau Stock hurried off to a neigh-
bour's apartment, where a score of elderly women gathered
every Tuesday afternoon to read horoscopes. Fritz Stock
and his daughter strolled slowly through the fading Spring
sunshine to Weissensee, where they sat down on a bench
under lime trees on the banks of a small, round lake.

"The city seems so quiet today," Christiane said.

"They're all down near the government buildings de-
monstrating against the raising of the work norms," Fritz
said. "That's where I would be if you weren't here."

"Was it bad in the prison, father?" Christiane said.

"I don't want to talk about it."

"Did they hurt you?"

"There was one man there ... Sauer ... an animal."
Fritz Stock fingered the welt over his eye. "But it's over now
They did let me go."

"Why did you do it?"

"Because I got tired of being taken for a fool, of being
lied to. I just got fed up. I'm fifty-six-years old and it
seems to me that I've been tricked and lied to for fifty of
those years. The Government announces a 'New Course'
and then they turn around and raise the work norms. *More
work for less pay.* And we're supposed to be doing it
voluntarily. It's too much. But I don't want to talk about

128

this. I don't see you often enough that I want to waste my time talking about such stuff."

"Father, I've been putting this off, but there's something I came over today to tell you. You might not see me again for a long time."

"What do you mean?"

"I'm going to be married. To an American."

Fritz blinked his eyes and stared at the little cup of blue water. After a long pause, he asked, "Is he a soldier?"

"Oh, no. He's a professional man. An engineer, I think."

"How long have you known him?"

"About a week."

"Christiane, are you sure of what you're doing? I've heard so many stories. . . ."

"He's a good man, father. And I love him."

"That's not always the most important thing in a marriage, Christiane."

"He's a serious man, father. He's older than I am ... a widower. He has a good position and a house in California."

"That's where you'll live?"

"Yes, near Los Angeles."

"Then I really won't ever see you again—"

"Father, please don't talk like that—"

"What am I supposed to do? My daughter, the only person I care a damn about, is going to be married and live in the United States and ..." Fritz Stock's voice rose and then trailed off.

"What would you have me do, father?" Christiane said, with a sad gentleness.

"Yes. That's it exactly." Fritz Stock's voice was very small now. "There's nothing I can say. There's no future for you here."

"You shouldn't worry, father. He's a fine man and I'm very lucky. He's the first man I've known who doesn't sneak around, evading things. I know he'd like to meet you."

"Would he come over here?"

"He can't do that. He works for the American government now and won't cross the border."

"Damn those borders," Fritz Stock said angrily. He paused to watch three green riot trucks, filled with People's Police as they raced past, heading for the inner city. "Look at that," he said. "It wasn't always like that. But you never had a chance to really know Berlin, did you, Christiane? You were born here and now you're leaving without even having known what it could be like. It used to be a good place, when I was your age, before the first war. Even after that, life was hard, but you could have a good time. All you've ever seen is rubble and uniforms and the rest of the *Schweinerei*. You've never seen the lime trees in bloom along the Unter den Linden...."

"Father," Christiane said. "Why don't you visit us in Dahlem?"

"How can I do that, Christiane? I'm a foreman on the project and if they found out...." Fritz stared at his hands. "The devil with it. I'll come over one night. When will you be getting married?"

"I don't know for sure. But it will be within two months. I'll have to apply for a visa and other papers, so I don't think I should come over here again. Will you tell mother?"

"I'll tell her. One of these days."

"I guess there's nothing more to say, then."

"No, there's nothing more to say." Fritz got up and kicked a stone into the water. "There's nothing I can say. It's a funny feeling to know that nothing you say makes a bit of difference."

Fritz put his arm around his daughter. "Don't pay any attention to me now, Christiane. I just realized I'm getting old. I do want you to be happy. If it only means that you'll be happy, it will be worth not seeing you again. One gets used to everything in life. When are you going back?"

"I have to be at the S-Bahn station in Gesundbrunnen at seven tonight. He's meeting me there."

"Then you can come back to the apartment now and have one last supper with us. I'll open a bottle of Rhine wine."

"All right."

But when they neared the apartment block, Fritz grabbed Christiane roughly and pushed her behind a heap of rubble. "Do you see that car?" he said. "And that man standing near the door? S.S.D. They've come to arrest someone. I don't want you to come in now. I want you to go back to West Berlin now."

"Father, why don't you come with me?"

"No. I'm staying here. They haven't come for me. They wouldn't have released me if they thought I was dangerous. But I don't want you staying here. I'll take you to the station."

Fritz accompanied his daughter to the S. Bahn station. He kissed her on the cheek as she got into the train. "Good luck, Christiane. I'll come over to see you next week." He stood watching the train until it had curved away from him into the dusk, then went downstairs and started to walk home. He normally walked with the jaunty, rolling gait of an old sailor, but now he walked slowly, head down, shoulders hunched.

He ducked into his neighbourhood *Bierstube* and had three quick shots of *Korn*. He heard voices around him, talking about the demonstration that day. It had been a great success, the Government had left the marching strikers alone, tomorrow there was to be a general strike. All the workers in East Berlin were to meet at seven A.M. in Straus-

131

bergerplatz. Fritz had two more shots of *Korn,* wishing that he had been with the marchers, then weaved out into the street.

He walked along, trying in vain, as he thought back on his life, to make something besides complete futility out of the sum total of the years : war; inflation; depression; the Nazis; war again (his three sons killed); his wife, her mind unhinged by the air raids, turned into a shrew; grubbing for bread in the rubble; Soviet occupation.

He had thought of these things before, but they had never oppressed him as they did now. He was not given to self-pity, and he considered himself luckier than most. His apartment had been spared in the air raids and in the last few years he had had steady work; two years before he had even been made a Hero of Work, presented with a medal and ten thousand East marks. He had thought he had learned to be thankful for small favours, to come to terms with frustration, and he wondered why he should suddenly be overwhelmed now by these feelings of anger and emptiness.

When he reached his apartment block, he saw that the S.S.D. car was still there. He turned off down the now dark street, under the cold stars, thinking of Christiane. In less than an hour he could be with her in West Berlin. But the thought of seeking charity from his daughter made his stomach turn. He decided to sleep in an abandoned cellar that night. In the morning, he would go to Strausberger-platz.

5

WHEN DAWN broke, Fritz Stock left the abandoned cellar where he had spent the night and walked, because the street-cars had stopped running, to Straubergerplatz, the huge square which formed the downtown anchor of Stalin Allee.

What he saw there surprised him and dispelled his dark mood. He had expected to find that a few thousand had had the courage to answer the general strike call; instead, every worker in East Berlin seemed to be milling about the square. It was a grey, overcast morning of the seventeenth of June, but the crowd seemed joyous, infected, not with a grim air of revolution, but with one of carnival.

A few People's Police watched with a curious, detached air as the demonstrators moved off toward Leipzigerstrasse at seven-forty-five. A heavy rain broke, soaking Fritz to the skin, but he pressed on, joining in the chanted slogans :

"Down with the norms!"

"Down with the Stachanovite methods!"

He noticed a worker holding aloft a sign that read : WE WANT LOWER NORMS! Still visible on its reverse side were the partially erased words : IN HONOUR OF MAY DAY BLOCK 0 HAS VOLUNTEERED TO RAISE ITS NORMS TO 10 PER CENT. Fritz grinned; he did not know where the marchers were going, or what they intended to do, but he had the wonderful feeling that at last something was going to happen. The strange procession, resembling a giant centipede with five thousand pairs of legs but no head, swept through Alexanderplatz; deep in its centre Fritz no longer felt helpless and alone.

He noticed that the People's Police were still making no attempt to interfere with the marchers, that no Soviet soldiers were in evidence. And he noticed that the demonstrators, their numbers swelling by the hundreds every minute, had begun to chant bolder slogans:

"Let the People's Government talk to the People!"

"Away with the secret police!"

"Down with the S.E.D.!"

"The Government must pay for its mistakes!"

"We don't want a National Army, we want butter!"

"Ulbricht, Pieck and Grotewohl!"

"We've had a belly full. . . ."

A sound truck appeared and raced up and down the length of the marching column, broadcasting the announcement that the government had decided to reconsider its decision of May 28 to raise the work norms by 10 per cent. Fritz joined in hooting down this announcement; nobody was thinking any longer of simply lowering the work norms; the original modest request which had touched off the demonstrations yesterday now seemed to belong to a forgotten time.

Arms linked, wooden clogs resounding on the pavement, the demonstrators pressed on, smiling, singing: *Brothers, toward the sun, toward freedom.* . . . Fritz sang along with them, and his heart sang, too, filled with wild hope; for the first time in longer than he could remember he felt alive, felt like a man.

As he entered Unter der Linden, Fritz noticed that stronger units of People's Police had appeared along the line of march, although they still made no effort to intervene; nearing Leipzigerstrasse, he saw that People's Police had blocked off the streets leading to the *Haus der Minist*

erien. The sirens screamed, trucks rolled up, and young
oldiers of the new National Army, in khaki uniforms of
oviet cut, leaped down upon the crowd, swinging trun-
heons. The air of carnival was replaced by a turmoil
f scuffling, blows, and shouts.

"Traitors! Throw your clubs away and join us!"

"You're workers' sons! Are you going to beat workers?"

"Shame! Shame! You're German, too!"

"Go home! We want no violence! Our claims are justi-
ed!"

Fritz was caught up in a confused, writhing mass of
odies. A truncheon flashed over his head, he felt a sharp
lancing blow, blacked out and came to on his hands and
nees. He was not seriously hurt, but tears welled up in his
yes. All the misery and frustration of his life seemed to be
ummed up in his present predicament, kneeling there help-
essly on the wet pavement, his head throbbing, aware that
e had been tricked again, that the demonstration was be-
ng broken up, that nothing at all had really been accom-
lished. Sick with rage, remembering another truncheon,
e got to his feet and shouted, "To the prison!"

In the tumult and confusion, there were a few answering
houts, "To the prison. We can't do anything here!"

"Free the political prisoners!"

"Release our husbands!"

"To the prison!"

When Fritz reached the prison that he had left the day
efore, he saw that it was guarded by a single platoon of
ery young People's Police, armed with carbines. They stood
n a thin, nervous arc before the entrance, faced by hund-
eds of angry, shouting workers, many of them holding
ieces of rubble and wooden planks.

"Let the prisoners out!"

"Throw away your guns and join us!"

135

"Let's storm the building. They can't shoot all of us!"

Fritz fought his way to the front of the leaderless crowd. "No violence," he shouted. "We don't want to bring the Russians into this. No violence. Let's have a committee of five go inside and talk to the warden. If the committee isn't out in twenty minutes, then you can take action."

His proposal was relayed to the sergeant in charge of the platoon, who relayed it to the warden inside. Agreed. The warden would make no promises, but he was willing to talk to a committee. Fritz and four other workers were selected to enter the prison, where they were escorted to a large office on the main floor near the entrance. The warden leaned back in a swivel chair, and regarded them over his desk top with an impassive expression. "Well, what do you men want?"

Fritz, remembering four days in a damp cell, a dog, a truncheon, felt his patience breaking. Fighting hard to remain calm, he said, "We want you to release all the political prisoners. The common criminals we don't care about."

"Impossible," Warden Sauer said. "With what authority do you speak?"

"With the authority of the People of Berlin."

Sauer snorted. "I'm afraid I cannot recognize such authority. Your request is denied."

"You have fourteen minutes. If the prisoners aren't released by then, there will be bloodshed."

"It won't be my blood."

"It will be, Sauer. That crowd is getting bigger all the time. They'll storm the building and those Vopos won't be able to stop them. Hundreds of these people have relatives in here. And they all know you."

Sauer got up, walked to the window, and peered out at the angry mass of people which had swelled to two thou

136

sand. "They're lice," he said, almost to himself. "They wouldn't dare. . . ."

"Twelve minutes, Sauer. If you act now, you probably won't be harmed."

A look, not of anger, but of puzzlement and indecision crossed Sauer's face as he stared at the thin arc of People's Police facing the huge mob. "But I have no authority to accede to your demands," he said. "All the high officials have been called away to a meeting of police chiefs."

"Ten minutes," Fritz said. "I'm warning you. We don't want violence, but if there is any, the blood will be on your hands. The prisoners we want released are innocent, and you know it."

"I must have time to think this over . . . to think. . . ." Sauer was almost pleading now. "I don't have the authority. It's too irregular."

"You've had enough time. Just give us the keys to the cells. I'll lock you up until the crowd leaves so that no harm will come to you."

"Let me at least telephone my superiors." Sauer was whining now. "If I don't tell them that I was forced to do this, they'll shoot me later."

"You can do anything you want to do. We just want those keys in eight minutes."

"I'll let you leave, to prove my good faith. I'll have you escorted outside."

"We don't want to go outside. We just want the keys. Hand them over—"

Suddenly Sauer darted away into the next room, locking the door behind him. Fritz and the four other workers pounded at the door with chairs, but could not break it down. Leaving the others behind to smash at the door, Fritz ran outside. As he was explaining what had happened, six riot trucks, with sirens screaming, came hurtling down the street. Leaping out of the way, Fritz thought: *the fool, he called them.*

A full company of People's Police piled out of the trucks and formed a triple cordon before the prison; the first line held rubber truncheons; the second, carbines; the third, machine pistols. A light machine gun was mounted on the steps, its snout staring down into the crowd. The lieutenant in charge of the People's Police strode up and down between his men and the demonstrators, apparently in confident command of the situation. "Go home, you people," he said, in an even voice. "Go home now and nothing will happen to you."

"Go home yourself," came the answering shouts.

"Throw away your guns and join us!"

"Release the political prisoners!"

"The twenty minutes are up! Release the committee. Give us the keys!"

The crowd, which outnumbered the Vopos a hundred to one, inched forward menacingly. "Go home," the lieutenant repeated, deliberately avoiding any tone of sharp command. His voice and manner were still controlled and authoritative, but inwardly he was racked by confusion and growing anxiety. His unit had been placed on combat alert at dawn and called in from Potsdam only an hour ago; he did not have a clear picture of what was happening. And yet he knew more than the demonstrators in front of him; he knew that he had strict orders not to shoot unless it became absolutely unavoidable, and he knew that riots like this had flared up throughout East Germany.

He wondered how he could avoid giving the order to fire if the crowd attempted to rush his men. A single volley, of course, would cut down hundreds, but he was sure that the Government did not want that to happen; yet, at the same time, he was sure that the Government did not want to have this prison sacked. Another thought added to his uneasiness. The crowd, growing larger and more furious with each passing minute, might keep coming and engulf his company even if he did give the order to fire.

The lieutenant did not like the idea of dying to defend something he did not believe in. He had joined the People's Police out of simple opportunism. He had entered the Wehrmacht at seventeen, fought throughout World War II as a sergeant, and then found it difficult to master a civilian trade in the chaos of post-war Leipzig. He had not regretted joining the People's Police (the pay was good, the uniform well cut, the routine life made him feel secure), but he had never thought he would have to face up to a situation like this.

Something queer was going on; he could not understand it. His commanding officer had told him briefly that he was to help in containing a minor disturbance of rowdies, fascists, and American *agent provocateurs,* but it was obvious as he looked into the crowd that it was made up of ordinary working class Berliners like himself. What would happen if they—and the millions who were rioting in the zone— really succeeded in taking over the Government; what would happen to officers of the People's Police then? He cursed the day he had become a lieutenant; as a sergeant he had only to follow orders; placing him in a situation like this was unfair.

He glanced at his men, but this gave him no reassurance. Most of them were teen-age boys, who looked neither competent nor determined. Some of them were grinning, others glanced sheepishly at their boots or fingered their weapons nervously. He wondered, his anxiety turning to panic, if they would obey an order to fire; he was a tough disciplinarian, he knew he was not liked and many of the enlisted men must have friends or relatives in the crowd. He paced up and down, his sober calls to reason drowned out now by the taunts and insults which made him their focal point.

"*Lump!* Traitor ! Swine !"

"You call yourself a German? You're a Soviet-German !"

"Shame ! Shame ! Will you protect murderers?"

Dear God, the lieutenant though, please don't let one of them lose his head and rush at me. He had decided to go to a riot truck and radio for reinforcements when he heard a great shout and turned around to see the door of the prison open.

One after another, four bodies, unconscious and bleeding, were thrown down the steps. Warden Sauer appeared and shouted out over the crowd, "There are your keys !"

An animal roar caused the lieutenant to spin around; the crowd was surging forward. He raised his arm in the agreed upon signal. He had only to drop it and the first wave of demonstrators would be shot down. Racked by confusion and indecision he hesitated, and while he hesitated Fritz Stock ran up and tackled him to the pavement.

6

DOWN IN the tomb of his cell, Sterling continued to hear the curious noises and then the entire cell block coming alive with rumours.

"War has broken out!"

"The Russians have attacked the Amis!"

"The Amis have dropped an atomic bomb on East Berlin!"

"The water mains have burst. We're going to drown!"

"The Red Army has mutinied!"

"The prison is on fire!"

He jerked to his feet, cracking his head on the low ceiling, and heard someone outside his cell door fumbling with the lock. Then the door was flung open and he was confronted by a wild-eyed, barrel-chested man in white overalls. Seeing him crouching there inert and bewildered, the man slapped Sterling across the face. "Run, man. Move quickly. We're setting the political prisoners free."

Sterling hobbled out into the corridor to find it swarming with running, shouting shadows whom he followed up three curving flights of stairs to the main floor. There he saw a score of men in front of a cell with a thick steel door which they were trying to break down with hammers, iron bars, bare fists. He knew he should keep going, but something stopped him and made him listen to the enraged shouts of the men.

"*Schlagt ihn tot!* Kill him!"

"Let him alone. The swine isn't worth killing!"

"No break down the door. He killed my brother!"

"Let's get out of here while we can. You'll never get that door open!"

"No! No! He's got to pay!"

"Make him throw out the keys! That's enough!"

"No! He's got to pay!"

But Sterling knew that he would not pay; locked behind that thick steel door with its ten-inch-square peep-hole, mocking his impotent besiegers with laughter and complacent threats of retaliation, Sauer was impregnable, indestructible. He had locked the exit door and then locked himself in his cell; he would remain safe inside it until help came; his besiegers were really the ones who were trapped. Like an incurable cancer, Sauer would enjoy his inevitable triumph, and his powerlessness before this mindless evil tortured Sterling more than anything that had yet happened to him.

He looked around frantically, until he realized that he was standing outside of a tool and die shop; seeing its floor strewn with cotton wadding and magnesium cuttings, his mind quickly formed and then gave way to a dark, barbaric plan.

He darted inside the shop and kneaded the magnesium cuttings and cotton wadding into balls which he doused with lacquer solvent. Fighting his way through the uncomprehending crowd, he called for a match, dropped the balls through the peephole and demanded the keys.

Immediately, the mocking laugh turned to a hysterical pleading whine; the keys were thrown out. Sterling picked them up and stepped back, his hands trembling and slick with sweat, wanting desperately to take the final step, but unable to do so. But he needed to do nothing more; as he watched in rigid horrified fascination, the man in white overalls pushed him roughly aside, set a match to a rag soaked in solvent, and tossed it into the cell.

Sterling flung himself away from the explosion of blue-white flame and ran off down the corridor, pursued by a soul-searing scream mingled with the piteous howls of a dog. Nearly retching, he fumbled open the lock of the exit door, and ran past men who were smashing filing cabinets, burning dossiers, herding disarmed guards into cells, out into the street where he saw armed soldiers in blue uniforms being embraced and kissed by a jubilant mob.

It took several minutes to collect his wits, to get used to the idea that something approaching a miracle was taking place before his eyes. He glanced frantically around, trying to orient himself; he was lost, but he knew that he was in East Berlin and therefore could not be very far from the sector borders. His mind told him that he should dash off in a westerly direction, that the only thing that mattered now was for him to find the border and cross it while there was still time. But he did not run off; his heart told him that he should stay and try to find Christiane.

He ran back up the steps of the prison, fighting against a stream of people who were rushing out of its battered doors, slowly realizing the senselessness of his action. If Christiane had been arrested and brought to this prison then she, too, would have been released by the demonstrators. It would be impossible to find her in this swirling mob, and she knew better than he how to get to the safety of West Berlin.

Reluctantly, he ran back down the steps and westward, but as he ran, his heart pounding, the cold rain reviving him, another thought caused a wavering in his determination to escape while there was still time. He remembered that he knew the name and location of the hotel where Doctor Winter was staying; from photographs, he even knew what the old man looked like. In this explosive time

143

where anything seemed possible, was there not at least a slim chance that if he hurried to the Johannishof he could find Doctor Winter and bring him over the border in the confusion? Torn by doubt, he had reached the Brandenburg Gate without coming to a decision.

He saw huge crowds swarming back and forth between the sandstone Doric columns of the gate; he had only to join them and in two minutes he would be free, in the British Sector. All around him people were singing, tearing down banners and photographs, burning newspaper kiosks. Crawling over the top of the gate, under the eyes of armed People's Police, two men were risking their lives in an attempt to replace the red flag with the Bear Flag of West Berlin.

The sight fascinated and decided Sterling. These crazy, wonderful people had released him from the hell of the prison, he thought; the least he could do was to summon up a fraction of their courage. He turned north, ran up Friedrichstrasse, and in ten minutes found himself before the Johannishof Hotel.

With bitter disappointment, he saw that it was guarded by People's Police. There was no hope that a man alone could slip past them, and since the hotel was of small importance to the rioters, they would not storm it as they had the prison.

Panting heavily, exhausted by running, Sterling could not go on. He sank to the ground and rested his back against a pile of rubble. The hotel (was Winter really inside, only yards away?) swam distorted by fatigue before his eyes; the precious minutes fled as he tried to recoup enough strength for his own final journey to freedom. Then, hearing a warning cry, he struggled to his feet, saw green armoured cars rolling toward him and the demonstrators running before them shouting :

"Der Iwan Kommt!"
"Russkis!"

Sterling, his lungs bursting, ran to Potsdamer Platz and saw that the sector borders were still open. He paused for breath near the burning H.O. Department Store and started his final dash when the riot trucks wheeled into the square. although he realized that this was inevitable, that the Soviets would not stand idly by forever and watch their prize satellite being torn apart, his immediate reaction was still one of agonizing shock as he saw troops piling out of the trucks, machine pistols pointed skyward, calling : *"Davay! davay! Hau-ruck! Hau-ruck! Geh Domoj! Go Home! Go Home!"* Within two minutes, they had sealed the sector borders with a methodical efficiency that had none of the hesitation of the People's Police.

Sterling dashed off to join a large crowd in a side street. A sound truck circulated slowly on the fringes of the crowd its speaker blaring over and over again : THE SOVIET CITY COMMANDER ORDERS : STARTING AT ONE P.M. A STATE OF EMERGENCY IS DECLARED. GATHERINGS OF MORE THAN THREE PERSONS ARE FORBIDDEN, VIOLATORS OF THIS ORDER WILL BE PUNISHED ACCORDING TO MARTIAL LAW. Three field-green T-34 tanks appeared at the far end of the street; their 85 mm. guns pointed skyward; officers in black uniforms stood up in their open turrets, motioning at the crowd, asking it to disperse.

But the crowd, goaded from sullen resignation into desperate defiance, refused to obey; it moved only enough to let the tanks pass, shouting up at the officers who stood in the turrets with impassive expressions :

"Ivan Go Home !"

"This is our city !"

"Our cause is just ! Leave us alone !"

"*Russki* go home !"

Two of the three tanks turned a corner and vanished, but the third swung around, its hatch slamming shut. Suddenly its machine gun began to fire short bursts high above the crowd's head, sending people flying for cover.

Sterling ducked behind a concrete subway entrance; he felt nakedly alone. If only someone would help, he thought desperately; if only help would come to these people before it was too late.

He looked up and saw that a stray bullet had ricocheted out of the rubble and struck an elderly woman in the hip. She lay wailing and writhing in the centre of the empty street as the thirty-five-ton tank, whose driver could not see what was before him at ground level, bore down on her slowly ... forty yards, thirty yards, twenty yards.

"*Schweine! Arbeiter-Mörder! Murderers of workers! Cowards!*" Men sprang out of the surrounding ruins, flinging rocks which bounced ineffectually off the armour plate of the oncoming tank. The helpless woman put her hands over her eyes and stopped wailing. The prow-shaped hull of the T-34 was almost upon her when Sterling dodged from behind his concrete sanctuary.

Snatching a rusted iron bar from the rubble, he ran, hunched over, to the left side of the tank. He thrust the iron bar between its wide metal treads and stuffed a blue denim jacket thrown to him by a striker into its exhaust, burning his hands slightly on the arrows of blue-white flame.

The T-34 swerved left, its diesel engine grinding and coughing to a halt, its disabled tread slapping angrily at the asphalt. Men swarmed over it, clawing at its hatch, as the sobbing woman was carried to safety. Then the other two tanks reappeared, machine guns chattering steadily just above the heads of the crowd, clearing the street.

Sterling hurtled out of the line of fire, into an empty side

146

street, just as a squad car occupied by three Soviet officers and three Germans civilians cruised past him. The car ground to a halt before a knot of people. Almost as though they were choosing him at random, the German civilians grabbed one of the strikers, hustled him into the squad car, and drove off. For an instant, Sterling thought that he recognized the arrested striker as the barrel-chested man in white overalls who had released him from his cell, but he couldn't be sure; so many of the strikers were dressed alike.

Well, it was over now, he thought bitterly, standing alone in the empty narrow street. The revolt that never had a chance had come to its inevitable end. It had failed, but he was still free. He was trapped within a city encircled by steel, but until he was arrested again, he still had a chance. Hearing the steady chatter of machine-gun fire in the next block, he plunged off in a southerly direction.

Peter Sterling did not succeed in crossing the sector borders that afternoon; he found every avenue of escape in the inner city blocked off by tanks and armed soldiers. He dashed into an H.O. store that was being wrecked and pillaged, exchanged his prison uniform for an inconspicuous blue denim work suit, stole a loaf of black bread and a tin of sausages, then lost himself in the centre of an angry mob that was being herded southeast along the border. He hurried across a bridge over the River Spree, recrossed it over another bridge lower down, and entered the suburb of Treptow.

In these outlying streets, the crowds were gradually broken up and dispersed. Sterling soon found himself alone; fatigue and hunger and fear of recapture in the dying afternoon light drove him to seek shelter in an abandoned air raid bunker. Here he drank rain water, smashed open the tin of sausages, wolfed them down with the black bread and rested until night fell.

He was about to leave the bunker, when he saw the match flare at its entrance. He snatched up a jagged piece of rubble, pressed up against the wall, and heard a man's voice: "Come on, in here."

The match went out and another was lit and heavy footsteps descended the stairs. "Come on," he heard the rough male voice repeat. "In here, in here."

Sterling, gripping the piece of rubble, could see the faint outline of the man's face in the light of the match. But he can't see me, he thought, not yet, not yet.

Then he heard a woman's voice: "No. Let's find someplace else. It's too dark in there, too damp. And there are always rats in these bunkers."

"But you promised!"

"I will, but I don't want to do it in there."

"Where then?"

"I don't know. But not here."

"All right. All right. Let's go."

Sterling dropped the piece of rubble; life, he thought, went on, even on a day of revolution. He waited ten minutes, then left the bunker. Dirt and a dark stubble of beard obscured the bruises on his swollen face; dark circles ringed his bloodshot eyes, but nothing in his body felt broken and it responded wearily to his driving determination to escape.

But time was running out, he told himself, and he was making pitiably slow progress on foot. If only he had some means of transport to speed this seemingly endless journey. He cursed his lack of a map, the risk involved in stopping at a strange house to ask directions, his ignorance of Berlin geography. But he knew that if he kept going south, then turned westward, he had to find the sector borders again.

He was walking slowly as he entered a quiet suburb identified by a sign as Baumschulenweg, convinced that he could never run again. He crept through a cemetery and at its end came upon a comfortable, isolated house. It was surrounded by a neat white picket fence, and leaning against that fence, just inside its gate, Sterling saw a bicycle.

It had hard rubber tyres, the kind that could cross any kind of terrain without puncturing, and looked more precious to Sterling than an armoured car. He decided to steal it; he could hardly afford the luxury of scruples in his situation, he thought, and the occupants of the house, judging from its prosperous appearance, were undoubtedly staunch party members. Best of all, the house, like all others in the suburbs on this night, was still devoid of lights.

The four-foot-high gate was locked, but he managed to crawl over it. The bicycle itself, he discovered with a rush of hope, was not locked. Very quietly he picked it up and was about to lift it over the fence when he was tackled from behind and heard a shrill protesting voice, "Papa, Papa! He's stealing my bicycle!"

The blood drumming in his ears, panic stabbing at his chest, Sterling kept his feet but could not shake the boy loose. He was about twelve years old and stockily built and tightened his chubby arms around Sterling's wobbly legs, shouting, *"Raüber! Raüber!"*

Lights flashed through the house, its front door swung open, and a huge fat man appeared on the porch. He was shirtless, wearing suspenders, and beneath those suspenders Sterling saw the blue trousers and jackboots of the People's Police.

The man stood staring down from beneath ludicrous square eyebrows at the two locked, wildly thrashing figures, vanished and reappeared in an instant with a furled umbrella just as Sterling managed to wrench free and start over the fence. He came barrelling down on Sterling, swinging the umbrella like a whip, but Sterling, still inside the fence, dodged away only to be caught round the neck by the man's fingers. Smelling the liquor-heavy breath, Sterling drove his elbow into the swell of the man's stomach and he fell back and to one knee.

Sterling was over the fence as the man got up and staggered inside the house. He'll call the local Vopo station, Sterling thought wildly, running, running. They have more to worry about now than sneak thieves, but if he gives them my description, and it matches the one that Benno has surely broadcast, they'll be after me like the hounds of hell.

He dared not keep to the empty streets now, and, punishing himself, he loped through the dark meadow of Königs-Heide and into the adjoining suburb of Johannisthal, where he almost blundered onto a heavily guarded Soviet airfield. He bellied into a shell hole, pressing his face down into the soil so that he could taste it between his teeth. He felt like a hunted animal, but also felt a hunger for final surrender and rest, a momentary death wish, that no animal ever feels.

But when he saw that he had not been noticed by the guards, he skirted the field, crossed a small foot bridge over a canal, and reached the suburb of Alt-Glienicke; with infinite longing he stared across at the lights of Rudow in the American Sector; all entrances to it were guarded.

He continued cautiously south through silent, moon-lit fields, dodging away from occasional patrols, cursing the never-ending labyrinthine land mass that made up greater Berlin, unable to orient himself by the few odd landmarks he passed : a monument to Kaiser Wilhelm II, view tower, a steamer pier, comfortable villas on the banks of a river.

The suburbs ended at last and he entered a wood of pine trees; as he walked on, the terrible feeling that he was getting completely lost swept over him. He was about to double back, although he knew that he could not hope to avoid the patrols for long with the coming of light, when he stumbled upon a wide ditch, on the opposite bank of which stood a ten-foot-high barrier of logs and barbed wire, interspersed by tall watch towers and searchlights at hundred-yard intervals. He ducked quickly behind a tree, hope draining out of him until he noticed that the great staring eyes of the searchlights were dead. He studied the watch towers and could see no sign of activity in them; incredibly, they seemed to be deserted.

He leaped into the ditch, waded through slime up to his hips and gained the barrier. He found it too high to scale, and too solid to break through without tools. But the loam beneath it was wet and pliant from the rains. He found a flat rock and began to dig; gnats bit at his neck and hands; in the distance he heard the faint barking of dogs. After an hour of furious effort, he had tunnelled out enough space for a man to crawl through.

He burrowed forward through the soft yielding earth, lay flat on his stomach for ten minutes gasping for air, then rolled over on his back. He saw the barrier, the ditch, and East Berlin behind him. He got to his feet and suddenly, frantically, began to run.

He ran and ran, an old nursery rhyme coursing through his brain :

Run, run, run, catch me if you can,
You can't catch me, I'm the gingerbread man.
I am, I am, I am.

When he was out of the dark pine forest and into a desolate open meadow, he stopped and looked back again. As he stood there panting happily, savouring the wonderful surging joy of freedom, of release, it began to drizzle. Shivering in the damp cool night, he forced himself to go on, alternately running and jogging and walking, until he saw a solitary half-timbered farmhouse about a hundred yards ahead of him; near it sagged a small, dilapidated barn.

Rain clouds blacked out the moon and he decided that now he was free, there was no point and some danger in plunging ahead aimlessly in the dark; when dawn broke, he could make his way easily and surely through these outlying West Berlin farm districts to Dahlem. He stole up to the barn, unlatched its door, and crept past three scrawny cows, softly whistling the nursery rhyme, wondering why he did so, where he had heard it before.

Then, smiling, he remembered. His father had once sung that song as they played hide-and-seek in a California garden. How wonderful it would be to be back there with Christiane, he thought, especially since he had emerged from the ordeal of the prison purged of his old anxieties. He made himself comfortable in a pile of hay, West Berlin hay he thought joyously, and rubbed axle grease on the burned palms of his hands. Thinking that he would be with Christiane in only a few hours, he had begun to drift off into a deep sweet sleep when the flash of lightning exploded next to his right ear.

Before he blacked, Sterling saw in a second of vivid intensity the butt end of a submachine gun and above it the grinning oval face of a soldier wearing a brown uniform and the blue cap of the M.V.D.

STERLING AWOKE to the warmth of sunrays slanting across his face. There was a lump the size of a tangerine behind his right ear; his head throbbed. He glanced around and caught sight of a short, round man in a threadbare brown suit several sizes too large for him, eyeing him from a distance of ten yards with the sinister scrutiny of a cat eyeing a bird. Looking at the man with crushing disappointment and rising horror, Sterling thought he had finally gone out of his mind. But as he stared at the man he slowly realized that he was not a halucination; he was Benno.

"Congratulations on your escape, Mr. Sterling," Benno said. "Where do you think you are now?"

Sterling did not answer; his eyes dropped and focused on the ·22 automatic held in a soft, celery-coloured right hand.

"I suppose you think that you're safely in the suburbs of West Berlin?" Benno continued. Sighing, he sat down, his wide flabby hips spreading over the sides of an overturned milk pail; somewhere, far off, a cock crew. "Unfortunately, you're in the Soviet Zone of Germany, in farming country near Königs-Wusterhausen. You must have crossed that zonal border near Schmöckwitz. The guards were temporarily withdrawn from there to help deal with the disturbances in the city. Mr. Sterling, you have escaped from East Berlin into East Germany. All that effort for nothing. Quite remarkable to have come this far, considering the condition you're in."

Sterling noticed a pitchfork leaning against the wall. Ten

yards away; too far. Five yards from him was a length of bicycle chain. If ge could get to it quickly . . . any risk, even the risk of being shot, would be worth taking to keep from being returned to the prison.

A hornfly settled on Benno's pudgy right cheek. Sterling tensed. Benno slapped it away; his steady gaze did not waver. "It must be a great disappointment for you," he said. There was no trace of sarcasm in his soft, purring voice. "One doesn't get a chance like that every day, eh? You really should have run across the sector borders before they were sealed off. There was plenty of time. Your guards are waiting outside. There are Soviet patrols all over this area. They found you last night quite by accident. But they had your description, because we gave it to all patrols. When they found you, they radioed for me. Now we are going to take you back to the same prison from which you were released. Only this time, there will be no escape. . . ."

Quickly, Sterling rolled toward the chain and—braving the expected explosion—whipped it at Benno's feet. Benno dodged aside by inches, but did not fire; he stood back, looked down at Sterling patiently, without anger. "That wasn't necessary," he said, in a curious voice. "Now get up and we'll join the soldiers."

The scrawny cows moved and lowed in their stalls; the cock crowed again. Sterling was on the verge of surrender now; he had few reserves left. The dreadful knowledge that he had come this far and failed exhausted him far more than any physical punishment he had undergone. Unresisting, shoulders hunched, he weaved out to the muddy barnyard, out toward the beginning of a silent and interminable night, with Benno padding behind him.

There were no vehicles about, but four soldiers, all very young and all armed with submachine guns, were waiting for them with bored expressions. One of them was a few inches over five feet, with a slight but wiry build, straight black hair, copper-coloured skin and oriental features. Benno snapped an order at him, relieved him of his sub-machine gun, and the soldier advanced on Sterling with handcuffs.

Seeing the handcuffs, Sterling summoned up his last ounce of resistance; anything, he thought, even death itself, would be better than going back to the prison; while this final slim chance was still open, he had to take it. He dodged away from the handcuffs and made a wild lunge for the weapon of the soldier nearest him.

Quickly, Benno raised his submachine gun, aimed it at Sterling's chest, then moved it away and pressed its trigger. There was a burst of orange flame and a chopping noise and one after another the four Soviet soldiers, almost torn in half by the slugs fired from point-blank range, pitched forward into the mud.

Benno ran up to Sterling who stood rigid, gaping paralysed, and slapped him across the face. "Listen to me," he said. "Listen to me closely. I killed them because I have decided to go to West Berlin myself. And I want you to help me."

"You're a lunatic," Sterling said, staring at the four still, mangled bodies; the mud turning dark red with their blood.

"No. It is you whose mind is unbalanced. That's understandable, considering what you've been through. But you are presumably an intelligent man, and you'll come to understand that I know exactly what I'm doing. I'm going to take you into the farmhouse now. Walk ahead of me. Quickly, we don't have much time."

Sterling, speechless with incredulity, his mind reeling, had no choice but to do as he was told. "An elderly couple lives here alone," Benno explained, as they entered the neat, simply furnished farmhouse. "Very fine people. Jehovah's witnesses. They gave me a fine breakfast this morning. We don't have to worry about them. They're out in the fields working. Now we'll start a fire so you can take a hot bath."

Benno, automatic in hand, watched over Sterling solicitously while he took a hot bath in a wooden tub, changed into a warm clean suit belonging to the farmer, and finally devoured a meal of pea soup, pumpernickel, sheep cheese and a tolerable steak of horsemeat.

While this was going on, Sterling, his shock thawing, became certain that Benno was indulging himself in some bizarre, maniacal cat-and-mouse game. He waited for an opportunity to jump him, but none came; he did, however, manage to slip a razor-sharp bread knife into his pocket.

They went into the living room and sat in wooden rocking chairs, facing each other over a low table, upon which were several copies of the *Watchtower,* a book called *Let God Be True,* and a Bible. Over the fireplace hung a framed quotation : "Before them the land lies like an Eden paradise, behind them it is a desolate desert."

Benno saw Sterling glancing at this. "Queer people, the Witnesses," he observed in a cheerful conversational tone, as though they were two old and good friends, passing the time of day in a comfortable country inn. "Branch Servant Julius told me earlier that Christ returned as King of the Earth in 1914, that the second coming had already begun to take place, and that the world as we know it will come to an end in our generation. The Witnesses actually believe this sort of thing, mind you, and they are prepared to suffer any kind of punishment for their convictions."

Benno paused and indulged himself in a not unpleasant

mile; Sterling noticed four stainless-steel false teeth in the front of his mouth. "The sect is banned in East Germany, of course," Benno went on, unhurried, "as it was under Hitler. Small wonder, since they refuse to recognize Governments or to bear arms. This farmer Julius actually spent four years in a concentration camp because he would not renounce his queer notions. Now he's on an S.S.D. 'undesirable' list, which is why the patrol searched here last night."

Benno took a pint bottle of Danziger Goaldwasser from his pocket, and two small water glasses from a cabinet. "Unfortunately, they do not drink. This belongs to me." He filled the glasses with a silver liquid with flecks of gold swimming in it, placed them on the table, and asked, "How do you feel now, Mr. Sterling?"

"Better." Sterling slipped his left hand into his pocket, clasping the handle of the knife.

"Take a sip of the Danziger," Benno said. "I will clear your head. I want you to have a clear head for what I am going to tell you."

Sterling hesitated. Benno noticed this, smiled, and drank from his own glass. "You persist in thinking that I mean you harm," he said. "Please believe me, Mr. Sterling. To me your health and safety are the most important things in the world right now."

Sterling's palm became moist around the knife handle. He tried to calculate; if he flung the glass of liqueur into Benno's eyes and leaped across the table, would there be time. . . ?

Benno glanced at his wristwatch. "I ask for ten minutes of your undivided attention now," he said. "I am going to be completely frank with you. I am an agent of the Ninth Section of the M.V.D. My work for the past twenty years has been in the field of political assassinations and kidnappings. I make no apologies for that. Once I'd started with this

157

work, it was impossible to stop. Since the death of Stalin some disquieting changes have taken place within the M.V.D. New people have come to power . . . some of whom regard persons of the Stalin era like myself with distrust and hostility. Recently, I heard that Beria himself had been arrested. Two days ago, I found out that this was no rumour but fact. Yesterday, during the confusion, I confirmed another rumour—that many of Beria's protégés were to be arrested. I was one of them. I know, better than most people, what arrest by the M.V.D. can mean. The uprising yesterday made me decide to take the lesser of two evils and defect to the West. Quite a few people in the M.V.D. and the S.S.D. will be in serious difficulty because of those foolish disturbances. That's what comes of taking a softer line. Nothing like that could possibly have happened if the old leader were alive. But I am straying from the point. Are you a good swimmer, Mr. Sterling?"

"Yes. Fairly good." Sterling's fingers tightened round the glass.

"Good." Benno smiled, rocking back and forth in his chair. "Well, then, I have an interesting proposition for you. I doubt if you can get back into West Berlin by yourself. But I know a way—probably the only way—to do just that. I am prepared to take you with me, if, once we are there, you will take me to the director of your organization and tell him who I am."

"You *are* a lunatic. Do you seriously believe that I would help you in any way?"

"Please, Mr. Sterling. Try to forget your personal feeling and be objective. I'm sorry that I had to question you under those primitive conditions. I don't like them and they rarely succeed with determined people, but I was in a hurry. And I'm sorry if I was responsible for your kidnapping. What would you have had me do when my superiors gave me

158

the assignment? Refuse? I am being objective and I only ask that you do the same. Collect your wits and try to understand what I am offering you. I am not only offering you your life, but I am offering your Government invaluable information about the operation of the M.V.D. throughout the world. Look at this."

Benno drew an oilskin packet from his inside coat pocket and tossed it into Sterling's lap. "You'll find there a fairly complete list of M.V.D. contacts and cut-outs and agents presently operating in Western Europe. And another list of officials of Soviet embassies and consulates in Canada and the United States who are registered as diplomats but who are in reality M.V.D. men. And many other things I was able to steal from our files during the confusion of the riots. What do you suppose such information is worth to your Government? It has no price. Look at it. Look."

Sterling was obliged to release the knife and the glass in order to examine the contents of the packet. He quickly saw that this was no trick; although most of the papers were in Russian, those which he could read in German and English looked authentic—and sensational.

"Why should you think that I am deceiving you?" Benno pursued. "I could have killed you in the barn and had done with it. I tell you quite frankly that I would have done so if you had been anyone but who you are. If you refuse my offer now, I *will* kill you. But I don't want to threaten you. I want you to agree voluntarily to help me. I want you to admit that you cannot refuse me. You know that your Government wants the information that only I can provide. And all that I am asking in return is political asylum."

Sterling knew now that he was not listening to a lunatic, yet his revulsion at everything Benno stood for made him hold back.

"You still doubt my sincerity?" Benno said, with a rush

of anger. "Very well, then, let's have done with it." He levelled the Beretta at Sterling's eyes, his index finger caressed its trigger. Then, with a contemptuous movement, he flipped the .22 into Sterling's lap. "There," he said, leaning back in his rocking chair. "I don't know what further proof of my good faith you can ask for. And while you're at it, please stop fooling with that bread knife in your pocket."

Sterling picked up the Beretta, saliva coming to his lips, and pointed its barrel at the swell of Benno's stomach. It was the second time in his life that he had been consumed by a wild desire to destroy another human being.

A gadfly settled on the whitened knuckle of his right index finger. Conscious of a faint sting, Sterling hesitated and in that second of hesitation, his murderous impulse evaporated, to be replaced by feeling of disgust, confusion, resignation. What has happened to me? he thought. Have they succeeded in reducing me to their level? He placed the Beretta on the table and said in a flat voice, "I'll listen to you."

Benno betrayed no sign of relief; his attitude seemed to be that Sterling had done the only sensible thing. He leaned forward, produced a map of Gross Berlin, and spread its sections out on the table. He came round the table, crouched next to Sterling, and said, in the brisk, competent tones of an experienced travel agent, "When dusk comes, we'll walk northwest through Gross Berlin along this road to Potsdam."

"Potsdam?" Sterling was immediately suspicious. "Isn't that the headquarters of the Soviet Military Administration? It must be alive with patrols."

"Of course, it's S.M.A. Headquarters," Benno said patiently. "But they won't be expecting refugees to come through that way, for that very reason. We'll stay off to the

160

right, close enough to the road to keep our direction, but not close enough to be seen. When we reach the autobahn entrance before Potsdam, we'll cut sharply right to Babelsberg. You see that thin blue strip? That's the Griebnitz See. They can't very well cover every foot of it from Neu-Babelsberg to Kohlhasenbrück. At this point, the waterway is no more than fifty or sixty yards wide. We'll swim across to the City Forest in Wannsee. To cross by land is out of the question. How does my plan sound to you?"

"I have no way of judging its merits."

"Believe me, this is the only way. We should have an easy enough time until we reach Neu-Babelsberg. That's a populated area and there will be patrols. Dogs, too, perhaps. I won't try to delude you that this is going to be easy, but if you do as I say, we have a chance. Unfortunately, I cannot swim, but I found an inner tube in the barn. You will help me there? I will float and you will pull me?"

Sterling nodded.

"Good. Now all we can do is wait for dusk. Would you like to sleep? Would you like more Danziger?"

Sterling shook his head. "You should understand that I can't guarantee what will happen to you when I bring you to my office. And you should understand that I personally hope that you will be turned over to West German authorities for hanging."

Benno refolded the sections of the map, returned to his chair, and began complacently to rock back and forth, his hands clasped in his lap. "Capital punishment has been outlawed in the Federal Republic," he said easily. "And there is nothing your officials can do to me in any case. There is no proof, anywhere, that I have committed any crime." He leaned forward. "Don't you think that I have taken all this into account? But why must I justify myself to you? I am not a sadist. I am not a criminal. I am not a

161

political fanatic. I was forced into this work. I myself am a victim, the victim of a terrible accident, carbon monoxide poisoning. When I was a young student of pharmacy, and an excellent one, too, an old countess in whose home I lived committed suicide by releasing carbon monoxide from her gas stove. The gas seeped into my room while I was sleeping, poisoning but not killing me. After that I found it difficult to concentrate on my studies for long periods of time. I was discharged from the university. I became incapable of any normal pursuit. I became incapable of sexual intercourse; I, who had once liked girls so much. . . ."

Benno suddenly uttered a mild oath in Russian, plunged his right hand downward, and began to scratch his crotch. His suit, made of a cloth called "worsted-cellulose" —a component derived from timber—had begun to itch abominably after having dried after the night's rain. "I joined the M.V.D. or the Ochrana as it was called at the time, simply because it was the only job offered to me. They found my studies in pharmacy useful. But I never enjoyed my work in the Ninth Section. I swear it. No, no. It was just a job to me. But I did it well. I did it well for twenty years—" his voice rose—"and look at my reward! They would have tortured me, as they did you! But they were always plotting against me . . . from the first, in Spain. They were envious of my ability. They never trusted me fully, never gave me the rank that was my due, because my father was a Volga German. Now I shall pay them back!"

Benno fell silent, sucked on the bottle of Danziger Goldwasser, and began scratching his crotch again. Watching this, Sterling had to stifle a grim smile and a wave of gruesome pity. The terrible part of it was, he thought, that he believed Benno's story. It was undoubtedly true that the man had become a professional killer out of no other motive than expediency, and would not hesitate to kill him, if the need arose, out of the same simple motive. Life meant nothing to the man seated opposite him, because his own life meant nothing. Benno repelled and embarrassed him, like a grin, he thought on the face of a corpse.

"Now that we're more or less partners," Sterling said dryly, "do you mind telling me what happened to Doctor Winter?"

Benno shrugged his shoulders. "Winter? I have lost all interest in that one. I never had any personal interest in him, just as I had no personal interest in you. The last I heard of him, he was still in the Johannishof. The great scientist was badly frightened and confused because the American agents never made their promised contact with him. He was not working with us. Poor man, he really did want to defect, though I can't understand why. They would have treated him like a king in Dresden."

Now Sterling asked the question that had been tormenting him for days, the question whose answer he must have. "How did you find out about our plan to defect Doctor Winter? Who told you?"

"Of what importance is it? Why talk about the past?"

"It is important to me."

"The girl told us."

"What girl?"

Benno looked genuinely surprised. "Surely you must have guessed. Gretel von Luttwitz, the adopted daughter of Baroness von Luttwitz, Winter's sister."

Sterling's heart raced. "Your certain of that? You couldn't be mistaken?"

"I'm not mistaken. As you may know, Winter is a wealthy man. On the other hand, the Baroness and her daughter have very little money. If Winter should die, the Baroness would inherit all of his property, his stocks, his patents. But the Baroness is old, in her seventies, and in delicate health.

Her daughter shares her vice of parsimony. Do you follow me? We also discovered that she is of weak moral character. She has engaged in various sordid liaisons with American W.A.C.s from the day the occupation began. We contacted her a year ago, when the decision to repatriate Winter was first made. We ignored the Baroness; she seems to have some genuine affection for her brother. But to the daughter—who was known to your authorities and carefully avoided—we made a simple proposition. We would guarantee that Winter would never set foot in West Germany alive if she would simply report to us on persons contacting her mother. She agreed to do this, if in addition we would pay her a small monthly sum and give her a fur coat. She was able to arouse our suspicions about this Hodesblatt. We watched his movements every day for a year. It was not easy; he was very cautious; his system of cut-outs was rather ingenious. But eventually, with perseverance, we were able to identify most of the people interested in defecting Doctor Winter."

"But why all those killings in West Berlin? They weren't necessary if you simply wanted to keep Doctor Winter from defecting."

"They had a definite purpose. Your organization has lately been causing us some concern. We decided to discourage your activities by creating a climate of terror, by undermining the morale of your personnel, by making each of your agents wonder if his identity, too, was known. We deliberately encouraged Winter to come to East Berlin so that your agents would attempt do defect him. Then we eliminated them one by one, and in your own territory, as an object lesson. At first it was planned to cripple you in a street brawl on your first night in Berlin, but then this plan was altered. We decided to kidnap you, to exploit to the full the propaganda value of putting an authentic

164

American spy on trial for all the world to see." Benno paused. "You still haven't escaped that trial yet, you know."

"What about Fräulein Stock? Did your men arrest her?"

"She never returned to her family's apartment. I have no idea where she is now. She went straight back to West Berlin, probably, if she has any sense."

Sterling's heart sank; he was possessed by a driving obsession to regain West Berlin as quickly as possible. His eyes travelled to a row of photographs on the mantelpiece; there were three photographs of young men in uniforms, the frames draped in black, and a yellowing photograph of the farmer and his wife. The strong, honest, toilworn faces stared back at him and he said, "It's getting late. Shouldn't the owners of the house be returning from the fields by now? How do you know that they haven't been questioned by a patrol or even gone to report us? And what if another patrol has gone to look for those four men you killed?"

"Because I radioed to my headquarters that they had made a mistake in identification. That you were just an ordinary refugee. And the people who live here are fine people. They wouldn't report us. I know that." Through the open window came the sound of a cow bleating, as if in pain. "You are very distrustful of people, Mr. Sterling. The inevitable result of engaging in espionage work. But I assure you that you have nothing to fear."

Benno rocked back and forth, and ran a hand through the few sparse pink hairs on his skull. "I said before that I do not fear punishment at the hands of your authorities," he continued. "But there is something I do fear—reprisals from my own organization. How well does your Government protect Soviet defectors like myself?"

"I wouldn't know," Sterling said. "I'm really not connected with this business in a permanent way. Thank God."

"But surely they will fly me to Washington, immediately, under guard?"

Sterling could not resist deriving pleasure from the revelation of this first crack in the other's composure, and playing upon it. "I doubt it," he lied. "For all I know, they'll question you and turn you back to the Soviet authorities."

Benno stopped rocking and leaned forward anxiously, toying with the onyx ring on the index finger of his right hand. "They wouldn't be so stupid," he cried. Then he checked himself, and smiled complacently once again. "You're trying to disturb me," he said. "Go ahead, I don't care. I know that the Americans will protect me. Others of our service have defected, and they have all been treated correctly. I know of one man and his wife who defected in Japan and are now living in a very nice home in Arizona, under permanent guard. I know of this because we at one time thought of dealing with this man, but had to abandon the plan because he was so well protected. He will be taken care of for the rest of his life. Of course, it is rather confining, but I would not mind that. I have had enough of travelling. And I would use the time to write a book about my experiences. I believe I could earn a good deal of money with such a book. Is Arizona a pleasant place?"

"Most of it is very hot and very barren."

"I shouldn't mind that. I like a dry hot climate. You see, I suffer from asthma." Benno blew his nose noisily on a handkerchief that had been improvised from a tablecloth. "You know," he continued, "perhaps I could earn additional money making lecture tours and denouncing some of your citizens who are bothersome to your Government. I don't care about money, though, you understand. But my dream has been to be a pharmacist. I would use the money to purchase a small pharmacy one day, in some small, out-of-the-way village. . . ."

"If you don't mind," Sterling said. "I have to relieve myself."

"You'll have to go to the privy outside, next to the barn. I'll wait for you here."

Benno made no attempt to follow Sterling; he had gauged only too well the strength of the bonds of expediency which now held them together. It angered and disgusted Sterling to know that Benno had accurately calculated his importance to S.I.N., the fact that he would be beyond punishment if he did succeed in reaching West Berlin, and the extent of Sterling's present dependence on him. And yet, despite the inescapable logic that told him he must go along with Benno's plan, Sterling still could not bring himself to believe in it completely; he could not rid himself of a sense of anxiety, a lurking fear that told him to be on his guard until this journey was completed.

He started to leave the privy, but heard a clattering metallic noise and immediately flattened himself against the wall. Had a patrol come at last? he wondered, a breath of panic stirring his skin. Hearing another odd noise, as of someone rooting around, searching, he peered through a crack toward the direction from which it had come.

With immense relief, he saw only an overturned milk pail and a large shepherd dog, whining and nosing frantically in a woodpile. But, as the dog succeeded in knocking aside several small logs, Sterling's relief changed to horror. Two booted feet were projecting stiffly from the pile, and he realized why the cows had been bleating in pain. They had not been milked, and for an obvious reason.

He ran outside and tore away the topmost logs, revealing the farmer and his wife laid out neatly on their backs in a tomb of wood. Their fully-clothed bodies were so rigid that they appeared to have frozen. Their eyelids had been closed, there was a greenish froth at their white lips, and their blue faces were contorted in expressions of agony.

Sterling looked away and was almost sick. He walked slowly back into the house to find Benno still rocking back and forth, calmly sipping the last of the Danziger Goldwasser. "You scum," he said quietly. "You murdered those people. A harmless old man and his wife!"

"So?" Benno betrayed no concern. "You found them, did you? But you are jumping to conclusions again. I did nothing to them. It was an accident. Something they ate. Perhaps ergot poisoning, deadly nightshade, any one of a number of things. Personally, I think they died from eating *Gyromita escula*. It's a form of toadstool. It's very tasty and quite common around here. The peasants often eat it, especially when other foods are scarce. Unfortunately, it contains Helvellic acid and must be prepared quite carefully before it is safe to eat—"

"It was no accident," Sterling said. How much of this, he wondered, could he endure? "If those people died of poisoning, you did it. I don't know how, but you did. And someday, somehow, you'll have to pay for that, too."

Benno stood up, stretched, and yawned. "Enough of this, Mr. Sterling," he said. "It's time we were off. We have a long hard journey ahead of us. It will be difficult enough without the added burden of this pointless bickering."

He waddled to the door and gazed out at the woodpile. "I don't understand you. Mr. Sterling," he said, and his tone sounded not mocking, but utterly sincere. "I do not understand how a man as intelligent as you are supposed to be can seriously entertain these primitive ideas of retribution, of morality. There is no justice, anywhere. Life is a futile, meaningless business, just one long, hard journey to the grave. People are not worth worrying about."

"Goddammit, that's not true! It's not true!" Sterling's voice was shrill. He fought hard to control his rage, and the awful knowledge that not so very long ago he had come to feel the same way as Benno did now.

"And why not?" Benno said easily, as though genuinely seeking an answer.

"Because of that uprising yesterday! Because of those people rising up against hopeless, impossible odds. People can't be all bad if such things can still happen—"

Benno held up his hand and shook his head wearily. "But that, too, was futile," he said. "The disturbances are over now and the jails are fuller than ever. Nothing has changed. Nothing."

"No!—"

"You're confused, Mr. Sterling," Benno broke in. "I suspect that you may be a hypocrite. You want desperately to escape, because you know what is in store for you if you don't, yet you refuse to admit to yourself that it was to your advantage that this unfortunate accident happened to the farmer and his wife. These people seemed trustworthy, but one can never be sure. Now we are sure. And then, what real difference does it make? They were so old. At least, now they will be spared the disappointment of failing to see the end of the world."

Benno saw Stirling staring at him, his face twisted with loathing, his body tense and coiled as though ready to spring, and broke off. He stepped quickly out into follow him, and called over his shoulder, "Before we go, I will milk those cows. There is no point in leaving them in pain."

Sterling hesitated, the rage slowly draining from his body. Then he stepped out into the grey June dusk, out toward the patiently waiting round figure. I have to go with him, he thought, shame and guilt shaking him like a fever; I have to go with him because there is no choice and my partnership with this man is more horrible that all the raw physical horrors I have survived.

8

BEFORE THEY began their westward journey, Benno and Sterling had one final difference of opinion.

"I want to carry those papers," Sterling said.

"Why?"

"I don't mind your carrying the automatic and the flashlight and that bread knife, but I insist upon carrying those papers."

"Mr. Sterling. Please."

"I won't go on if you don't hand them over."

This one is against me, too, Benno thought. *I wonder if it is really worth it to bother with him. I need him until we cross the river, but then, after that ... perhaps.... He* sighed and handed over the oilskin packet. Then, draped in the farmer's too large suit, with a patched inner tube hanging around his neck, he padded off into the twilight.

Neither spoke as they moved steadily and easily through a faint mist, patches of marsh and bog, orchards, and low-lying plains with deposits of sand, with the sounds of summer for company: the croaking of frogs, the worried chirping of a mother sparrow, the sound of damp wings being flapped free of water, the hum of mosquitoes.

As they approached a sluggish stream, they were brought up short by a curious, whimpering noise. A wild-eyed roe was writhing in agony, one of its legs caught in a steel trap. Benno slipped out the bread knife, and slit its throat with quick expertise. "The cruelty of these peasants is unbelievable, even in this day and age," he said. "Those traps have been outlawed in the Mark for years, but they persist in using them." He shook his head, wiped the blade clean on a handful of grass, and said, "Now we'll have to get a stick and test all the rest of the ground ahead of us. There may be more of these wretched things, and it's possible that there are still some buried Teller mines left, too. Let's go on, but walk carefully."

Sterling felt a great sense of relief when their steady progress was checked at nightfall as they came out of a forest of gnarled and bushlike pines and saw circles of light moving back and forth in the dark. "Ahead must be the Potsdam entrance to the autobahn," Benno said. "Wait here while I crawl forward to see what's going on."

Fifteen minutes later, he returned. "There are vehicles all over the autobahn," he whispered, "but no foot patrols seem to be bothering about the surrounding fields. Our situation is good. If we can't see them from here, they can't see us." A faint burst of machine-gun fire echoed through the summer night. Benno shook his head. "Someone trying to cross by land," he said. "It can't be done."

Hunched over, they crept with nerve-racking caution and slowness into the outskirts of Babelsberg. Sterling was soon startled to find himself creeping past a plaster castle, a Norman village, and down the empty street of an American frontier town, complete with saloon, blacksmith's shop, and jail.

"This used to be part of the U.F.A. film studios," Benno explained, as he led Sterling out of the maze of mouldering sets, under the elevated railway of the Potsdam-Griebnitzee S-Bahn, and into Rosa Luxemburg Strasse.

"This is madness," Sterling said. "Walking through the streets like this."

"We have no choice. There is no other way to reach the

172

river bank. I don't think they'll expect anyone to defy the curfew order. Anyone in the streets at this hour is to be shot on sight."

Benno's judgment proved to be correct; the streets through which they passed were silent and deserted as those of a ghost town. At last their footsteps turned from asphalt to grass as they started across a field pitted with shell holes, and approached the thin strip of water that was their goal.

Here their luck ran out. With bitter, sickening disappointment, Sterling saw a fire blazing in the mist a hundred yards in front of them. Huddled around it were four soldiers in brown uniforms; another soldier, a machine pistol and a pair of binoculars slung around his neck, trudged up and down along the bank. Sterling stared at the fire, and at the other fires flickering all along the length of the river. Five against two, he thought; it was worth trying, except that any noise would surely bring soldiers from the other posts down on them within minutes. His hands trembled, and he almost cried with frustration.

"The end of the journey," Benno said grimly. "Let's go back to the Zone. We can hide out in the fields for a week or so and try again when the sentries have been withdrawn."

"The hell with that," Sterling said. It took a great effort to keep his voice low. "Let's try further up river."

"No. It widens out too much. I could never make it, even with this tube."

"But I can."

"I doubt it. No matter how good a swimmer you are. And if you try to desert me, I'll call out to the soldiers. Don't forget that as yet no one knows that I intend to defect. I could tell my Section that you forced me to come here."

From the campfire came the sound of a strong tenor singing: "*Kak, khodel, gulal, Vaniusha. . . .*"

173

"Well, they're Russians," Benno said. "Probably from the Fourteenth Mechanized Infantry Regiment. Experienced, dependable troops, not like the People's Police. More bad luck. Let's take our chances in the zone."

"No," Sterling said. "There must be another place around here to make an attempt. There must be—"

"No. Here is our only chance." Benno suddenly thrust his onyx ring under Sterling's nose. "But I'll tell you one thing, Mr. Sterling. I won't be taken alive. This ring contains a cyanide capsule. Here—" He handed the Beretta to Sterling—"take this, and use it if you're caught. Don't let them take you alive."

From the campfire floated the sound of other voices joining the tenor in violent song, punctuated with loud bursts of laughter. Benno peered through the mist and whispered, "They sound as though they're getting drunk." As he peered and listened intently, his expression, which seconds before had been one of utter dejection, brightened. "They *are* getting drunk. They must have stolen some *Schnaps* during the riots. That means we still have a chance. You see those bushes off to the right! We'll crawl over into them and wait. In a few hours they'll be so drunk that you'll be able to knife whoever is on sentry duty."

"Knife him?"

"Yes, yes." Benno handed the bread knife to Sterling; its sharp blade was still flecked with dried blood. "I'd do it myself, but I'm not strong or agile enough. And I can't swim. I need the extra time to get into the water with the tube. It will only take you a second, and before the others have collected their wits, we'll be halfway across. In their drunken state, and in this darkness and mist, they couldn't possibly hit us with machine pistols or submachine guns. The things are only accurate at close range."

"I won't knife anyone. I've had enough of killing."

174

"Please, Mr. Sterling, please. This is neither the time nor the place for another display of ethics. If those soldiers saw us, they wouldn't hesitate for a second to shoot us down like dogs. Now let's go."

They snaked forward unnoticed into the bushes, which were only fifteen yards from the bare river bank and twenty yards from the campfire. They could see the soldiers in the light of the fire, laughing and singing; they were all very young and disinterested in anything around them except the bottle of *Schnaps* being passed from hand to eager hand. At five minute intervals, the sentry passed within a few yards of the bushes; he seemed to be performing an onerous chore, and displayed no inquisitiveness at all. But, as the minutes lenghtened into hours, a new and unexpected danger arose.

The damp chill of the summer night turned slowly to bitter cold. A biting, bone-chilling wind swept in over the water. Lying rigid in the wet grass, without underwear and with only the flimsy protection of his tattered shirt and linen slacks, Sterling began to shiver; although he had always thought it only a figure of speech, his teeth now began literally to chatter. He had never in his whole life felt so cold, not even in Sauer's 'Bathtub,' and it was only by pressing both hands over his nose and mouth that he could prevent himself from sneezing and coughing. He was wondering how much more of this new torture he could endure when Benno inched over to him. "Come," Benno whispered, stretching out his arms. "We must keep warm."

It was the final irony, Sterling thought as, with arms locked around each other, bodies crushed together, their hot breath in each other's faces, he and Benno lay in the bushes like a strange beast with two backs, waiting.

At four A.M., the sentry was replaced by a short, chunky,

very young soldier. He trudged back and forth, a bit unsteadily, his large feet wrapped in the strips of cloth known as *portyanki,* a grey army blanket over his shoulders, singing softly to himself : *"Sygray pro otchy karye. . . ."*

"He's drunk," Benno whispered. "He's been swilling at that campfire for hours." Far off, the barking of dogs could be heard. Benno's eyes narrowed. "Dobermans," he said. "They'll be here in five or ten minutes. We can't wait any longer."

Suddenly the soldier turned around, left the river bank and walked with a rolling, bandy-legged gait toward the clump of bushes where Sterling and Benno lay, fumbling with the buttons of his fly.

Coiled up in the soft sandy soil, Sterling saw him coming; despite the numbing cold, sweat formed on the palms of his hands. The barking of the dogs became more distinct. Benno slid the inner tube around his wide hips, dug his fingers into Sterling's arm and hissed. "Now. Now." Sterling drew the bread knife from his pocket; its cold metal burned like hot ice in his hand. He waited, frozen, until the sentry stopped a few feet from them and started to perform the natural function that is the inevitable result of hours of drinking.

If only he had not seen his face, Sterling thought. It had been different with Sauer, but now the necessary quick savage mindless hate was lacking. Standing there with his legs spread in a very human attitude, singing softly to himself, this young boy did not look like an enemy, the final barrier to freedom, but a helpless fellow human being.

Without a word or a signal, Benno rose up and bolted past him for the bank. Sterling rocketed up, the knife flashing over the round, wide-eyed face. How simple and swift it would have been to drive the knife home, but he could not do it. He dropped the knife, brought his knee up in the boy's groin and darted for the bank. Diving after the floundering Benno, he caught hold of the inner tube, and pulling it, swam with quick strong side strokes toward the opposite bank, forty yards away.

The sentry scrambled to his feet and lunged, doubled over, to the bank. Through the throbbing pain, the confusion, and the alcoholic mist, he made out the two figures thrashing away—in slow motion, it seemed—through the black water. He readied his submachine gun and cried out, "Stoi! Stoi!"

But they did not stop. The sentry, as he had been taught on the firing range, applied a slight pressure of the trigger; there was a jolt and a burst of orange flame as a line of slugs—the first of seventy-two rounds—chopped up the water in front of the two men, who were so close together that they seemed to be one.

"Stoi!" he cried again, sure that they would obey, sure that they realized that they could not get away. But still they did not stop. Again the slight pressure, the jolt, the orange flame, this time followed by a wail of pain, so hideous and unearthly that it made him pause as his comrades came running stumbling up to join him.

Benno was knocked under the water by the impact of the slugs that shattered his right arm and tore apart his inner tube. He bobbed to the surface, gasping like a fish out of water, water pouring from his mouth, thrashing his arms and legs with furious futility.

Sterling treaded water, succeeded in catching hold of his left hand, and then saw his face lit up in the sudden shimmer of flashlights. Benno's face was no longer an expressionless mask; now it was alive with emotions: disbelief, pain, but most of all a terrible fear.

With a sudden, illuminating shock Sterling wondered how many faces had shown that same terrible fear when they had looked into Benno's eyes. What evil thing, he thought, was he now risking his own life to preserve; what justification could there be for it?

"Hold me," Benno gasped. "Hold my hand. Don't let me go...."

Quite deliberately, Sterling released Benno's frantically grasping left hand, dove under the water, and swam through the blackness until his water-choked lungs and eardrums seemed about to explode.

When he resurfaced, half way across, but a million light years from his goal, the sentry saw him quite clearly, bracketed in the little pools of light cast by the flashlights of the other soldiers. He aimed his submachine gun; all it would take now would be one slight final pressure. But in a rush of confused alcoholic thoughts, he remembered the knife striking toward his jugular; the knife that the fleeing man could have plunged home, but had not. Lowering the snub-nosed barrel, he emptied the magazine into the water below the man's kicking feet until he was under the water again and then out of range.

When he had dragged himself up the west bank, Sterling did not run. He did not need to run, he thought, he was free. And yet he felt no wild surge of exhilaration, of thankfulness, of intense relief. He only felt very tired and conscious of the fact that he would no longer have to run.

He looked across the dark water and saw five soldiers standing there in the shadows, some of them unsteadily, grinning at him. One of them made a quick obscene gesture with his fist, called out something in Russian, threw his head back, and laughed. The others began to laugh, too.

Sterling turned and started back through the Berlin City Forest toward Dahlem. He would always remember the last thing he saw before doing this: two of the soldiers, stripped to their underwear, descending gingerly into the Griebnitz-

See to fish out the body of Benno, who, writhing and screaming, was still very much alive.

When Sterling had dragged himself to the villa on Hindenburgstrasse, he found its door locked. Fighting to keep from fainting, he rang the bell and rang again and the door opened and he pitched forward into Christiane's arms. He slumped to the floor and lay on his back, his head cradled in her arms, as she kissed his forehead, the face swollen and bearded and caked with dirt. "My God, my God," she said softly, kissing him, pressing him to her. "Where have you been? You look like you've come back from the dead. . . ."

"I was dead," Sterling said, as he lost consciousness. "I was, but I'm not anymore."

9

"WELL," HARRY CHUTE said, smiling down at Sterling lying in the hospital bed, "you'll be out of here tomorrow."

"Out of where?"

"Out of the hospital. They claim that there's nothing wrong with you that a few weeks' rest won't cure. Although I must say, looking at you, that's hard to believe. Just as soon as you feel up to it, we're flying you home. I hope that will be within a few days, because Washington is very eager to talk to you about your ... uh ... experiences."

"But what about Uncle Max?"

Chute shrugged his shoulders. "Who knows? It's going to be a long time before we can even try to begin to find out what happened to him. One result of that uprising was to seal off most of our communications with the Eastern Zone." Chute glanced at the wall clock. "I'd like to stay longer," he said, "but I've got a million things to do at our place of business. We're going to have to close up shop and look for another location fast. Besides, you have another visitor waiting for you in the corridor and she's prettier than I am."

"Harry, I don't want to leave Berlin right away. I've got reasons."

Chute shook his head doubtfully. "They'll have to be awfully good. But let's talk about it tomorrow." He waved goodbye and hurried toward the door.

Christiane appeared immediately after Chute had left.

She paused uncertainly in the doorway, then almost ran to the side of the bed, paused again and kissed Sterling gingerly on the forehead.

"I know you can do better than that," he said.

"But are you all right?"

He sat up and took her in his arms, drawing her down to him gently. After several minutes, he released her and said, "Does that answer your question?"

"But what happened to you, Peter. How did you get like this? Were you in an automobile accident?"

"It was sort of an accident, but it had nothing to do with automobiles."

"Why are the windows barred and why is there an MP outside your door? You haven't done anything wrong?"

"Would it make any difference to you if I had?"

"No."

"I haven't done anything wrong. But it's too long a story to go into now. I'll tell you about it on our first wedding anniversary. Did you see your parents?"

Christiane's face, radiant with joy, turned melancholy, pensive. "I saw them," she said. "Then I took the S-Bahn back to West Berlin. I waited for you for hours on the station platform. Then I came back to the house, and waited and waited. I didn't know what to do or to think. Once I called Ray Duffy's number, but there was no answer—"

"Christiane," Sterling broke in suddenly, "do you think your father was one of those rioters?"

"He must have been. Knowing him."

"You don't know what's happened to him?"

"No. And I can't find out now. He might have been shot or arrested. Or perhaps he's still in Prenzlauer Berg, ready to go back to work. But I'm sure he was in the riots. Like everything else he ever did, it turned out to mean nothing."

"Don't say that, Christiane. Believe me, it did mean something. Look, when things have quieted down and they re-open the sector borders, I'll try to find out what happened to him. I have some friends that might be able to do that. And if they want to come, I'll try to arrange to have your mother and father live near us in California."

"Do you really care that much?"

"I care that much about you. And in a way I can't explain to you now, I care about them."

Outside in the street could be heard the hammering of pneumatic drills; bright thin poles of sunlight filtered through yellow-green leaves and the open barred window. Christiane sat next to Sterling, holding his hand, talking gently or simply sitting there in silence until dusk came and they became two shadowy figures and the nurse came in and said that visiting hours were over.

Three weeks later, Sterling found himself back where he had started, sitting in front of the desk of the Chief of Scientific Division in the Headquarters Building of the Secret Intelligence Network. Nothing had changed here: the faint hum of the air conditioning unit; the world stereo-scopic projection map on the wall; the scores of civil servants going to and fro on their arcane business in the grey corri-dors outside; the granite face of the Chief looking at him over piles of documents labelled with varying shades of secrecy.

The only change that Sterling could note was in the Chief's attitude toward him. Whereas before he had re-garded Sterling in a brisk, icily-efficient manner softened by a rather patronizing paternalism, he now beamed at him with admiration, with something approaching awe.

But Sterling had gotten used to this. Since his return to Washington a week before, he had been the object of curio-sity, congratulation and interrogation "in depth" by platoons of experts; he had even been summoned to an hour's audience with that very busy man who was the Director of the Secret Intelligence Network. Sterling bore all this with a patient good humour that shielded his inner sense of grim amusement, for while he knew that his successful interrogation of Doctor Eitelfritz Winter had reflected great credit on S.I.N., he wondered just how many people knew how it had come about.

For Doctor Winter, during the first frenzied confusion of the seventeenth of June, had had the good sense to slip away from his guards into a surging, rock-throwing swarm of rioters and simply scurry down Unter den Linden, through the Brandenburg Gate and into the British Sector. He had taken a taxi to Berlin Military Post Headquarters, and asked the MP at the gate to bring him to a representative of the American intelligence service. The MP had nearly chased him away as just another in the daily parade of cranks, then had reluctantly called out a Counter Intelligence Corps sergeant, who had telephoned a Military Intelligence lieutenant, who had called an Office of Naval Intelligence Commander, who had called an Office of Special Intelligence colonel at Tempelhof, who had taken Doctor Winter into custody for a day and then called Harry Chute at S.I.N.

Doctor Winter had been flown out to Frankfurt with Sterling, who had interrogated him in a pleasant, isolated hunting lodge in the Taunus Mountains. There Sterling had learned everything there was to know about the twelve-thousand-h.p. turbo-prop engine of the Soviet Bear Bomber designed by Doctor Winter and other members of the Junkers-B.M.W. Collective, and had also learned that the Germans had been repatriated because they were no longer needed; Soviet engineers were now more than capable of proceeding on their own.

Doctor Winter was paid his thirty-thousand dollars and

bade farewell. He sold his Dahlem house and moved to Essen, where he became the technical director of a company manufacturing turbines for hydro-electric power. His sister, the Baroness, kept house for him, while her adopted daughter vanished into the Eastern Sector of Berlin, where she was reported to have married an important official of the Peiping Trade Delegation.

But the coup that had caused an even greater surge of interest at S.I.N. was the oilskin packet which Sterling had salvaged from his journey with Benno. Its contents more than made up for the inconvenience of having to reorganize completely the Berlin Base of S.I.N., change its cover, shift its location, transfer its American personnel, realign its network of foreign agents. The documents had proved to be an intelligence source of inestimable value which seriously hampered — however temporarily — M.V.D. operations throughout the world.

And Peter Sterling of all people, a rank amateur, the Chief thought, had brought it off. He beamed broadly across his desk and gave voice to an idea that had been slowly forming in his mind. "Pete," he said, "have you ever thought of making intelligence work your career?"

"No," Sterling said. "No, I haven't."

"You should," said the Chief, firmly. "We need men like you, Of course we can't afford to pay you what you're making in private industry, but we could get you a damned high rank and there would be all the other satisfactions ... public service, overseas field trips, knowing what's really going on in the world. I don't expect you to answer now, I just want you to think about it, seriously."

"I don't have to think about it. The answer is thanks, but no thanks."

The Chief shrugged; a pity, he thought. "Well," he said, "I guess you are pretty well fixed out there in Pasedena. I suspect that you'll be back at your job on Monday."

"No, sir. I'm taking a two-week vacation to sell my house
in Arcadia. Then I'll resign and go back to Caltech for six
months or so. I've got some money saved. . . ."

"The hell you say." The Chief looked genuinely baffled.
"That will mean going back to where you were ten years
ago. Why, if you come with us, we'd be glad to foot the bill
for your going back to college. We do it all the time with
our technical people."

"I know you do, Chief, but I really don't want to get
into intelligence work on a permanent basis. I really don't.
I know exactly what I want to do with my life and this
Caltech thing is just the beginning." Sterling paused, shift-
ing uncomfortably in his chair.

The Chief watched him sitting there in thoughtful silence,
realized that there was not the slightest hope of persuading
him to work for S.I.N., and changed to a more cheerful subject. "I understand you're getting married, Pete?"

"That's right, to a girl I met in Berlin. She's still there,
and having a little trouble getting a visa. The consulate
maintains her father is a Communist, despite the fact that
he's in a communist jail right now because he was in those
June 17 riots. But Harry Chute said that he was certain he
could do something about the visa."

The Chief rose, and came round the desk. "If Harry can't
do anything, just let me know," he said. "I'm pretty good at
getting action. And please accept my congratulations. You
did a splendid job, splendid. It's a shame, though, that you
couldn't have brought that agent of the Ninth Section over
with you alive. Are you sure that wasn't possible?"

"I might have been able to do it, but I don't think it's a
shame I didn't."

The Chief gave a hearty laugh and clapped Sterling on
the back. "No criticism intended," he said. "Well, I guess

that this is unfortunately the end of your brief career in intelligence. At least you can't say it was dull, eh? Must have been quite an experience to have been right in the middle of that uprising. Took us completely by surprise here. Russians, too, I'm sure. I somehow have the feeling that we could have taken advantage of the situation, done something to help. Don't know how, or what. It's too late now, though. In this business you can only get one turn at bat."

"Yes," Sterling said, eyeing the door. "It is too late."

"Well," the Chief said, putting his arm around Sterling's shoulders and escorting him out of the headquarters building, "at least you saw something unique. Take it from S.I.N., nothing like that uprising will ever happen behind the Iron Curtain again."

"You might be surprised. There are still some men left in the world."

Sterling waved goodbye and walked off—off into the summer sun, the cool breeze blowing through the Kwanzai cherry trees, the swarm of tourists converging on the Lincoln Memorial. He flagged down the first passing taxi and told its driver to hurry to the Wardman Park Hotel.

"Got to catch a train, sir?"

"No. I'm just in a hurry to make a transatlantic telephone call."

"Where to?"

"Berlin."

"Berlin?" The driver looked at Sterling in his rear-view mirror. "I was over there right after the war. Second Armoured. Now that is quite a town."

"Yes," Sterling said. "It is."

THE CASE OF
THE VAGABOND VIRGIN

by Erle Stanley Gardner

No. M.726

Why was Veronica Dale arrested on a charge of vagrancy,
when she had an hotel room booked in her name? And
was there any truth in the newspaper story that Addison,
who booked the room for Veronica after having given her
a lift, did not have the innocent motive that he professed?

Between the platinum blonde Veronica and the voluble
Addison, Perry Mason finds quite a pretty problem to
solve. For Mason can't quite decide whether Veronica is
as dumb as she seems, or whether she got herself arrested
on purpose. Addison, chief of a department store, is being
blackmailed for his part in the affair and is sore and mean
about it.

There seems rather more in it than at first appears—
and suddenly there is murder, and one of the most unfor-
gettable trial scenes in Perry Mason's career.

192 pp. 2/6

BAMBOO AND BUSHIDO

by A. G. Allbury

No. W.G.304

This is the story of a prisoner who did *not* escape, but who remained for three years in the hands of the Japanese, first in the labour camps of Singapore, then on the Burma Railway.

Mr. Allbury, a Gunner in the 18th Division, tells his story factually and without embellishment, but with no detail omitted. His is a saga of endurance that reaches a terrible climax when his troopship, en route for Japan, was torpedoed, and thirteen hundred P.O.W.'s were left by the Japanese to die in the South China Sea.

The author, very close to death after six days without food or water, was the only survivor on his raft and the last of the small handful of men picked up by an allied submarine. His account of almost unbelievable suffering and heroism is deeply moving in its simplicity.

256 pp. 2/6

TURN ON THE HEAT

by A. A. Fair
(Erle Stanley Gardner)

No. M.823

The last time Donald had seen Mrs. Lintig's little girl Evaline, she was a good-looking blonde about twenty-two, wearing wrinkled orange pyjamas—and a slightly annoyed look due to his rude awakening.

But that was the last time and Evaline wasn't good-looking any more, or annoyed. She was back in bed, but she wasn't likely to get up for anyone.

She was wearing a neat narrow cord drawn tightly around her neck.

It made her look a lot older than twenty-two—and it made her very, very dead.

192 pp. 2/6

THE CASE OF THE
DUBIOUS BRIDEGROOM

by Erle Stanley Gardner

No. M.942

Erle Stanley Gardner is a man of immense energy who keeps five secretaries working full-time. For twenty years he was a lawyer, but he eventually found practising law by day and writing by night was too much for him, so he concentrated on crime fiction. His total sales exceed 90 million copies, and he has written the record number of 50 books featuring Perry Mason, the lawyer whose daring legal tricks always save his clients. In *The Case of the Dubious Bridegroom,* a girl steps into Mason's office over the window-sill from the fire escape; and so begins a case in which murder enters, with a climax in a brilliant court-room scene.

Perry Mason is the hero of the B.B.C. TV series which scored such a success.

192 pp. 2/6

DOCTORS FOR HIRE

by Arthur Shaw

No. H.895

Arthur Shaw is a medical agent. As such he has been in a remarkably privileged position to observe the men and women who are qualified to put up a brass plate and practice medicine. Here they all are—the gay and the gallant, the diligent and the dissipated, the frail and the feckless: doctors all, and all brought to lusty life in this book.

For example, there is the missing doctor who was found naked and yet very much alive on the bank of a river; and another who caused a bit of bother when they found lipstick on his pillows—and he a bachelor; and a third who rode a horse on his rounds and preferred archery to arteries.

This basically is a light-hearted book and guaranteed to bring smile after smile to anyone who has been at either end of a stethoscope.

224 pp. 2/3

EAST OF EDEN

by John Steinbeck

No. VS.503

There is no more impressive writer in the world today than John Steinbeck, and *East of Eden* is probably his finest work. Set in his beloved California, Steinbeck's epic and dramatic story is reprinted by World Distributors for the first time completely unabridged, in a cheap edition.

East of Eden has won acclaim from the critics on both sides of the Atlantic, and was made into a tremendous motion picture starring the late James Dean, Raymond Massey, and Julie Harris in the leading roles.

Steinbeck's colourful and violent strength combined with his realistic harshness and knowledge of people, makes this novel a great one.

576 pp. 3/6